The Protectors Series

SLOAN

BY

Teresa Gabelman

The Protectors Series

SLOAN

Copyright 2016 Teresa Gabelman

All rights reserved. The right of Teresa Gabelman to be identified as the author of this work has been asserted in accordance with the Copyright, Designs and Patents Act 1988. This is a work of fiction and any resemblance between the characters and persons living or dead is purely coincidental.

Gabelman, Teresa (2016-9-28).

Sloan (THE PROTECTORS SERIES)

Paperback Edition.

Editor: Hot Tree Editing

Photo: www.istock.com

Cover Art: IndieDigitalPublishing.com

For The Readers

Chapter 1

Sloan leaned his head back, letting the steaming water beat against his worn body. Anyone who said a vampire couldn't feel was dead wrong. While he couldn't get an illness and he didn't need sleep, his mind, however, was past exhaustion. Dealing with the same shit day in and day out was enough to drive a saint insane—not that he was a saint. Far from it. Even in the shower, he could hear his phone incessantly ringing. He had tossed it on the bed in the room he more or less lived in. Despite having a high-end apartment overlooking the Ohio River, he was rarely there. No, he pretty much lived in the tiny room off his office at the compound.

With a grunt, he squeezed his eyes closed and tried to block the ringing of his phone as he shut off the water. Grabbing a towel, he stepped out of the shower without drying off as his cell went silent. Relieved with the brief reprieve, he walked into the small room that consisted of an unused bed, some of his clothes, a table he threw his shit on, and that pretty much summed it up. His phone rang again. Tensing, he let it go to voice mail, something he was doing more of.

Sitting on the bed, he rested his elbows on his knees and stared at the ground, trying to muster whatever in the hell he could to walk out his door into the madness he was sure waited for him on the other side. Once again, he found himself wondering if he had made a mistake so many years ago. Should he have died rather than making a deal with the devil, as that was what it seemed like? His life consisted of protecting others. Though deep inside, he knew his team were slowly losing that battle.

No one knew his feelings. None of his Warriors would *ever* know his feelings. He lived them alone, keeping them hidden; he was very good at doing just that. Finally lifting his head, he stared at the door as his body dried in the cool air. Maybe today would be different; maybe today they would make a difference in the war he and the others had agreed to fight. Not only was he in charge of the Cincinnati Chapter of Warriors, but he was also the eldest council leader. That meant everything went through him. It was too much for one man to handle, but handle it he did. He expected nothing less from himself and neither did the rest of the council or the Warriors who served under his leadership.

He felt old. Hell—who was he kidding?—he was old. Being turned at thirty-eight, he'd thought at that time he'd been too young to die yet, and being in a thirty-eight-year-old body did not help his aging mind. Sloan chuckled at his thoughts; he was slowly going insane.

Hearing voices, he grabbed his jeans. With a curse, he stood and tugged them on, dried off his short dark hair, and then wrapped the damp towel around his neck. Snatching up one of his many black T-shirts, he opened the door, once again hoping the day would be different than the last.

The sight before him pretty much summed up his reality—it was going to be the same shit, different day. Sid sat in a chair with his feet propped up on his desk as Damon stood against the wall with his arms crossed, looking pissed off as usual. Jared was texting wearing a goofy-ass grin, indicating it was probably Tessa he was messaging, while Duncan worked through a file, focused and serious. Sloan's gaze moved to Adam, who looked bored but gave him a nod. His eyes finally landed on Jax, who sat with Caroline on his lap as they whispered to each other.

"It's six thirty in the fucking morning." Sloan's voice broke the silence as he eyed each one of them. "What in the hell are you doing in my office?"

"Rise and shine, boss." Sid grinned, his feet rocking back and forth on Sloan's desk.

"Get your fucking feet off my desk," Sloan said with a growl, his eyes narrowing.

"Never were a morning person, were you?" Sid smiled but dropped his feet to the ground.

Caroline stood with a bright smile. "I don't know what they're doing here." Caroline frowned at the group. "But I'm here to make sure Becky feels comfortable."

Sloan's eyes shot to the small desk set up in the back corner of his office. *Fuck!* "Today isn't a good day," he didn't hesitate to say, but once his eyes met Caroline's, he knew he was fucked. Today was going to be *the* day, whether he liked it or not.

"She's probably already on her way here." Caroline crossed her arms over her chest, trying to appear intimidating, but it just made her look cute. "You've already postponed her start date twice, Sloan. She needs a job, *this* job. And you need help."

Sloan snapped the towel from around his neck and slammed it on his desk. "No, what I need is for you guys to get the hell out of my office."

Ignoring him, Caroline walked beside his desk near the wall where Damon stood and stared down at the floor where stacked files leaned precariously. "So, if I were to ask you for something, you could pull it out of that"—she pointed to the files—"without a problem?"

"Of course." Sloan didn't hesitate, yet he knew he couldn't. He didn't even know what was in half those files because he hadn't been through them.

Sid covered his mouth with his hand, coughing, "Bullshit."

Sloan gave Sid a dangerous glare before his eyes went back to Caroline. "I have gotten along just fine without any help."

"Just give her a chance, Sloan." Caroline offered him an encouraging womanly smile. "If she doesn't work out, fire her."

"Oh yeah, and then I'll have a distraught female crying all over the damn place." Sloan put his shirt on with a growl. "This is a no-win situation for me, as usual."

"Ah, man, stop being a Debbie Downer, dude." Jared snickered. "You never know, you might get lucky and have a secretary with benefits."

Caroline grabbed a file and smacked Jared with it. "That was a guy thing to say."

Jared just cocked his eyebrow at her, but his grin remained.

"You know—" Sid began, but Sloan cut him off quick.

"No, I don't fucking know and I don't want to know anything you have to say." Sloan sat, wishing like hell his phone would ring, but of course it was silent. Dammit, he couldn't catch a break.

"I was just going to say we should all get out of here," Sid continued as he stood.

"Now that's the smartest thing I've heard anyone say so far," Sloan murmured as his eyes took in his cluttered desk.

"So he can get dolled up for that sexy redhead secretary of his." Sid had already headed out of the danger zone away from Sloan.

"I knew Sid didn't have anything smart to say." Jared snorted as the rest hid their grins.

Sloan rubbed his forehead, wishing for death; he even glanced at Damon, wondering if the big son of a bitch would just do him the favor of decapitating him. He'd even pay him. As those thoughts swirled through his head, his door opened and the voice he heard had him reaching to see exactly how much money he had in his wallet to pay Damon.

"I'm back, bitches." Steve walked in the door, his smile spread across his face. "Miss me?"

******

Becky rushed around grabbing stuff and shoving it in her bag. She hated to be late and late she was going to be if she didn't get her ass in gear. Running to the bathroom, she snatched her mascara, dabbed it in and out to get the black goo on the brush and then stabbed herself in the eye.

"Shit!" Becky stood frozen, one eye squeezed shut. "Dammit, that hurts."

Finally able to open her eye, she wiped the black smudge off her face and continued at a slower pace. Once finished, she fluffed her hair, frowned, and then left the bathroom. It was as good as it would get. Caroline had said her position required casual dress, which was a good thing because casual was about all she had in her closet. Since her divorce, anything and everything that she could sell, she sold. Her main concern was to make sure her son was set for college, so he didn't have to worry and he had a fair shot of getting his life started. It was slim pickings at her house, which was fine with her. She was finally content, except for the fact she'd struggled to find a job so she could continue to pay bills and eat.

Locating her bag and keys, she headed out and locked the door behind her. Once her bag was secured to her scooter, Becky hopped on and said a prayer it would start. When it did, she said another one for no rain. She wasn't a religious fanatic, but prayers seemed to be about all the help she could get lately.

She had already ridden from her rental house to the VC Warrior compound three times to make sure she knew exactly how long it would take her. Twenty-five minutes wasn't too shabby, as long as it didn't rain, but on those rainy days, she didn't know what she would do. She had sold her car to pay her bills and only had an old scooter to get her around. So far it had done its job. She didn't have to hit any highways, but the bridge she had to go over into Cincinnati from Newport was going to be a scary experience during rush hour. She had only completed the trial rides late at night.

As she putted along the dark roads heading toward the river, Becky had time to think, and that wasn't a good thing. Filled with nerves, she focused on not shaking because it made her weave. She couldn't believe she was going to work for Sloan Murphy. He was an intimidating man, but just a man. Well, actually, he wasn't just a man. He was a vampire. A highly acclaimed vampire, from what she had read and heard. But she had made it easier on herself. Even though he was probably the sexiest man she'd ever laid eyes on, she had already made a pledge to herself that if she got lonely and needed a relationship, she was going the girl route. No more men. It was lesbian all the way. She gave a definite nod at that thought as she approached the bridge.

Checking her mirrors, she merged with the traffic. A few drivers honked, another flipped her off as she slowly crossed the busy suspension bridge, known as the singing bridge because of the humming sound it made when driven across. The bridge spanned the Ohio River between Covington and Cincinnati. It wasn't the safest route, but the fastest and she loved crossing it, except she was quickly changing her mind as the traffic whizzed by her.

Brake lights lit up in front of her and she slowed, keeping an eye on her mirrors to make sure the car flying up behind her saw her. Once stopped, she took a moment to look down. She could see the river through the bridge's steel grate deck. Because she'd never crossed during busy times, she had never paused on the iconic bridge, made famous for its debut in the movie *Rain Man*. It made one feel insignificant, looking down and knowing that all that separated her from certain death was a steel grate.

The sounds of a horn directly behind her had her looking up to see the traffic was moving. Once again she was on the move and becoming more nervous the closer she got to the VC compound.

Finally crossing the bridge safely, Becky breathed a sigh of relief, then headed down side roads that contained less traffic. Before she knew it, she was parking in front of her new place of employment. Reaching up, she went to take off her helmet and realized she had forgotten to wear it. Nausea hit her hard; okay, this wasn't good. She had to get it together and make damn sure Sloan Murphy didn't regret hiring her. Her forgetting something as important as her helmet was not a great start to a very important and life changing day for her. She was finally able to restart her life without her ex breathing down her neck. She'd have her own money and no one to tell her what to do with it. Yes, life changing, and she was more than ready. Nervous, but ready.

Unstrapping her bag, she looked up at the imposing compound. She had stepped inside only once before for her interview with Sloan, but had been so nervous she hardly paid the building any attention. Putting her keys in her bag, she continued to stare as she headed up the steps to the door, then gracefully missed a step and tripped. Stopping, she closed her eyes, cursed, calmed herself, and then continued. At the door, she did a quick assessment of herself before reaching for the handle. When the door didn't open with a twist of her wrist, Becky frowned. Glancing at her watch, she cursed again. She was only five minutes early. Raising her hand, she knocked and waited, and waited.

"Dammit." Her stomach twisted and burned. She was going to give herself an ulcer if she didn't chill out. She started to raise her hand again, but in her peripheral vision, she caught sight of a button. She had totally forgotten about the intercom system. Glancing up, she saw the camera—that she had also forgotten about—and knew without a doubt someone was watching her every move. Damn, the last time she was there, she really must have had her head up her ass. It was a surprise she was hired at all.

"Yeah?" a deep voice finally echoed through the early morning, scaring the shit out of her.

"Ah, it's Becky Spencer." Becky's voice wavered, making her roll her eyes and clear her throat. "I was told to be here this morning at seven."

She heard the click of a lock. Stepping inside, she once again felt insignificant as she found herself alone in a large entryway. A door to her right opened, which she did remember was Sloan's office, and out walked Caroline.

"You made it." Caroline smiled, hurrying toward her.

Glancing at her watch again, relief filtered through Becky. "And right on time."

"You're fine." Caroline waved her hand, dismissing her worry. "Come on. We have you all set up. Jill and I are going to give you the rundown, well, Jill mostly, but I'm here for support."

"Thank you," Becky said, meaning every word. She had been worried she was going to be left alone with Sloan right off. Discovering that wasn't the case calmed her nerves somewhat, until she walked through the door that Caroline had exited. It was a full house, and everyone was staring at her.

"Becky, this is… everybody." Caroline laughed with a shake of her head. She started to introduce the group as she pointed. "That's Damon, Jared, Duncan, Jax, Adam, Steve, and of course you know Sloan, Jill, and Slade. Sid ran off somewhere, but I'm sure you'll see him soon enough since he's always in trouble and in this office. You'll also meet the mates sometime today, I'm sure."

It was overwhelming to say the least. Each Warrior assessed her and she honestly didn't know if she passed their assessment of whatever she was being assessed for. She felt it was safe to nod and smile, which she did before looking back at Caroline, who was frowning at everyone.

"Stop it!" She pointed first at them, before looking back at Becky. "I'll definitely be teaching you how to block."

"Block?" Becky knew she had to look as confused as she sounded.

"Yes, block." Caroline led her toward the back of the room. "Because every Warrior in here is reading you right now."

Becky had to think about that for a minute as Caroline led her to a small desk in the back corner of the room, then gasped. "You mean, they know what I'm thinking?"

Caroline nodded. "It's annoying as hell, but you can block them."

"How?" Becky needed the skill immediately.

"Well first off, think of a naked man," Caroline said with a grin. She was loud enough for everyone to hear her. "That usually does the trick."

"The only naked man you better be thinking about is me." Jax cocked his eyebrow at Caroline from across the room.

Becky felt the blush rise from her neck, heating her face. Her eyes met Sloan's, who was staring at her, his eyes giving nothing away. She quickly looked away repeating to herself that she no longer found men attractive.

Chapter 2

Sloan half listened to what was going on, his eyes shifting to his new secretary. His trust of anyone was limited to his Warriors, and that was a trust they had earned after many years. He didn't get in her head because he hadn't had to. His background check, private investigator as well as his own searching gave him more ease, but trust her... not even close.

Jill started to head over to help Caroline with Becky, but he stopped her. "This better not backfire," he warned.

"Give it a chance, Sloan." Jill frowned. "When have I ever let you down?"

"Well, there was that one time—" Steve put up one finger as if counting.

"Shut it, lover boy," Jill snapped.

"Yeah, about that." Sloan glared at Steve. "I sent you to Kentucky in replacement of Dillon because—"

"I begged." Steve sighed dramatically but then straightened. "I did save Hunter's lady, though. That should count for something."

Sloan had heard all about it, actually about everything, but he had a bad feeling he was about to hear it again Steve style. Jesus, save him. He had sent Steve to Beattyville, Kentucky, to help the Lee County Wolves with their transition. Dillon had been directed to go, but the Warrior section Dillon had been working with previously needed him back, so when Steve had begged to go, Sloan gave in and sent him. Sloan had held his breath the whole damn time Steve was there representing him.

"So, you know I kissed a girl," Steve said with a shrug an d then chuckled. "Hey, that's a song by Katy Perr—"

"Steve, focus." Jared snapped his fingers in front of Steve's face. "Seriously, you don't want to fuck this up." He nodded discreetly at Sloan, who was staring straight at him.

"Anyway, Leda is old enough and well, they were just like… NO!" Steve shouted the "no" with a frown. "You know?"

"No, I don't fucking know." Sloan's eyes narrowed. "I do know that I got a call about having one less Warrior returning before I was questioned on how to kill a vampire because said vampire had his tongue down some shifter's throat who was under Garrett's care."

"Oh, ha, that Garrett is a funny alpha." Steve shrugged it off with another uncomfortable laugh.

"Garrett was a pissed alpha," Jill added from the back of the room. "And if it wasn't for Hunter, you'd be dead, like in wolf food."

"Don't need your help, Jill," Steve warned, then grinned at Sloan.

"Obviously, you do, Steve." Jill shook her head and then headed toward Becky and Caroline.

"But he tried to choke me to death, which you obviously can't do with a vampire." Steve snorted but cut the snort short seeing Sloan's glare. "So anyhoo…."

Jared outright laughed while Damon rolled his eyes. Duncan actually chuckled, and Jax stood and walked toward Caroline, shaking his head.

"Anyhoo?" Sloan felt the vein along his temple protrude; he seriously felt the fucker pulsing as if it were its own entity. "Did you fucking eat lead chips when you were little?"

"That's a big possibility, sir." Steve nodded, his facial expression indicating he knew he was digging himself into a deep-shit hole here and had no idea how to climb back out. "But I seriously meant no disrespect with Leda, and I did do my job with just a little fun on the side. I mean haven't you ever, you know, on the side with a nice piece of as—"

"If you even finish that sentence, I will pull my Carrie shit on you, and you will find yourself out in the parking lot without your feet touching the ground," Jill warned from the back of the room with a lift of her hand.

Sloan shook his head, but his eyes once again landed on Becky, who was watching the scene with a half grin. "I have shit to do, so brief me later. I've already talked to Garrett so I know everything already."

"Ah, okay." Steve looked disappointed. "I mean, what does that mean?"

"It means get the fuck out of my office." Sloan's tone was just below a roar.

"Who in the hell parked that pussy ass—whatever in the hell it is—in front of the compound?" Sid walked in, his face full of disgust, with Blaze following him. "No, better yet, which one of you guys turned pussy?"

"I'm afraid to ask." Sloan sighed for at least the hundredth time since he'd walked out of his small room into madness. "What in the hell are you talking about?"

"Well, thank God you ask because then obviously it's not you." Sid pinched the bridge of his nose. "Because honestly, if you turned pussy and started riding not just a fucking scooter, but a bright pink fucking scooter, I'd have to quit on the spot."

Sloan's eyes roamed the Warriors. Then his eyes fell on Becky, who looked guilty as hell.

"So who's the fucking pussy?" Sid demanded. "Hmm? Because you seriously need your ass kicked."

"That would be me," Becky replied, taking a tentative step forward.

******

Well, it was a positive way to start her new job. Being called out by one of the Warriors for being a pussy and standing out front with every single one of them, even Sloan, staring at her scooter was not how she'd thought her first day would go.

"Yeah, this isn't cool." Jared shook his head, then looked over his shoulder out onto the street.

"Hell, no, it's not cool," Sid griped with a growl. "We have a reputation to uphold here, and this is not healthy for our badass reputation."

"I'll move it." Becky had actually grabbed her keys out of her bag as she'd followed everyone outside to stare at her beat-down scooter.

"You crossed the bridge on that?" Sloan glared down at her, his frown menacing.

"Yes." Becky nodded, wondering how else he thought she'd arrived, since to cross a massive river you had to use a bridge. Though, she wasn't brave enough to be a smartass yet and say that. Instead, she climbed on and then stared up at Sloan, who still frowned at her. "Where do you want me to park it?"

"At your place," Sid replied, still looking disgusted. "Seriously, how safe is that thing? I suggest you drive your car from here on out."

"Don't have one," Becky said, feeling totally outnumbered. Even Jill and Caroline were looking at her scooter oddly.

"One what?" Sid asked absently as he leaned down, looking at the back tire of her scooter.

"A car," Becky replied, then laughed. "Listen, this is so not a big deal. I promise to park it off the property if I have to, but it's my only means of transportation right now."

"It is a big deal because it's not safe to ride that across the bridge during rush hour." Sloan's voice stopped anyone else from saying anything. "And where is your helmet?"

Dammit, of course her new boss, unless he fired her over the scooter, would notice the lack of helmet. "I kind of forgot it."

Sloan took three steps and with surprising gentleness helped her off the bike. "Steve, take it around back and park it."

"That's okay," Becky said, but let Sloan lead her away from her scooter. "I can do it."

"Sweet!" Steve rushed to sit on the scooter, then noticed Sid and the rest staring at him. "Hey, call me a pussy, but I think it's pretty cool. Can I take it for a spin?"

Becky wanted to hug Steve. "Sure, but be careful. She's old."

"Don't worry." Steve started the scooter with a big grin. "Old ladies like me."

"Jesus." Sid shook his head while chuckles and snorts filled the air.

"What? They do." Steve frowned and revved up the struggling engine; it sounded like it was ready to stall any minute. "Hey, Adam, you want to ride?"

"I'll pass." Adam shook his head, a half grin on his face. "You look right at home there, bro."

"Why thank you, Adam." Steve turned and headed out of the parking lot, but made sure to flip them the bird as he left on the bright pink scooter.

Chapter 3

Sloan led Becky inside toward his office. When Jill and Caroline tried to follow them, he held up this hand.

"I got this." Sloan started to shut the door on their protests.

"But, I need to show her—" Jill attempted to push it open.

"Come back at lunch, Jill." Sloan managed to close the women out. He headed toward his desk, but stopped and locked the door. He knew Jill well and she would find any excuse to come inside. He turned to see Becky staring at him wide-eyed. "Have a seat."

Becky sat in one of the two seats in front of his desk. "Listen, I'm sorry about the scooter. I didn't know it was going to cause a problem, but it really is my only means of transportation."

Sitting behind his desk, Sloan cursed to himself. How in the hell did he find himself in these situations? He didn't need a secretary, especially one who stirred feelings inside him that hadn't been stirred in more years than he could count. He didn't have time for this shit, but when he'd realized she had ridden that damn deathmobile in the dark, during rush hour, and across the river on one of the busiest bridges connecting Kentucky and Cincinnati, every protective instinct inside him demanded he do something about it.

"This isn't going to work." Sloan acted on his protective instinct with his normal bluntness.

"Excuse me?" Becky's head snapped back.

Before Sloan could respond, his phone went off and someone tried to open his door, then began to knock. Holding his finger up, he answered his phone and ignored the pounding on the door.

"Sloan," he answered, his voice harsh.

"You got your pick yet?" Douglas McGeary's voice boomed in his ear.

"I haven't had a chance to look, but it's the first thing I plan to do this morning." Sloan rubbed the bridge of his nose. He hated for anyone to rush him for anything.

"Well, dammit, Murphy!" Douglas shouted, annoyed. "I've got leaders up my ass wanting more men and I promised you first pick, so fucking pick already."

I said I will have my choice this afternoon, so shut the fuck up, McGeary." McGeary was a standup guy, but way too fucking intense for him and that was saying something.

Becky pointed to the door when Sloan glanced at her, but he shook his head. She just shrugged and sat back letting whoever pound, continue to pound.

"I need a pick as soon as possible, Sloan." Douglas calmed down some, but his voice still held an edge to it.

"Well, if you don't let me off the fucking phone, how in the hell do you expect me to do anything?" Sloan was getting more and more pissed off, to the point of hanging up on the son of a bitch, but he was doing him a solid giving him first pick.

"You got the files?" McGeary questioned.

"Yes, I have the files."

Becky pointed to the files piled and scattered beside his desk. Some had actually gone under his desk, because his feet kept sliding on them. He nodded and then watched as she started to bend toward the files. *Fuck!*

"I'm hanging up now and will call you this afternoon when I told you I would call you." Sloan hung up, then snapped his head toward the door. "Go the fuck away or die!"

That stopped Becky from reaching for the files as well as the pounding on the door. "Can vampires get high blood pressure?" She frowned, looking at him concernedly.

"No," Sloan replied, his eyes going back to her.

"So what files do you need?" She started to bend back toward the files, but he stopped her.

"Listen, Jill did this whole secretary thing without my consent and...." Sloan had no clue on how to fire someone. Well, he did, but not a beautiful woman. He usually just told whoever he wanted to fire to fuck off and not come back, or literally, he'd kick their ass out.

"So, you're going to let me go because of my scooter?" Becky's head tilted as she stared at Sloan. "Listen, Mr. Murphy—"

"Sloan." Nobody called him Mr. Murphy because he'd smack the fuck out of them if they did. Yeah, he was that cranky.

"Oh, ah, Sloan." Becky cleared her throat. "I need this job. I promise not to ride my scooter. I had no idea it would be such a big deal. I will take a taxi, get an Uber driver or something."

Dammit, if Jill were a man, he'd kick her ass. The knocking started once again and had him wanting to roar. Before he could, Becky stood and held her hand out, stopping Sloan before he could say anything, and then walked to the door.

Unlocking the door, she opened it a crack and looked out. "He's closed." Her voice was strong and sure. "Unless it is an emergency, come back in half an hour."

Sloan couldn't help the grin that lifted his lips. His grin widened when he heard Sid's voice after she closed the door and headed back to her chair.

"What in the fuck does she mean, he's closed." Despite the

soundproofed room—it took more than walls to prevent him from hearing curses and grumbles—Sloan heard Sid. "What is he, a fucking bank? Closed, my ass. What the fuck is this shit? He gets a secretary and now he's closed."

"Give me a chance, please." Becky had sat back down and was staring at him with the greenest eyes he'd ever seen. They were large with long thick lashes. "At least until I have another job lined up."

Sloan sat silent, he even tried to read her, but couldn't. She was a fast learner and had a block up. Before he could say anything, she started again.

"I'm not like most of those other women who showed up that day for interviews. I don't want nor do I need a 'Warrior.'" She did air quotes with her fingers. Then she snorted. "The last thing I need is a man."

He held in a chuckle as her eyes widened.

"No offense," she quickly added.

"None taken." He kept the smile from his face.

"I truly needed, *need* a job," she finished, her voice filled with hope.

"Do you have other job opportunities?" Sloan asked, leaning back in his chair.

"I have my resume in so many places I lost count. I'm just trying to get back on my feet," Becky replied, looking hopeful. "I'm not above begging for this job, Mr.... ah, Sloan. But I am not looking for handouts either. If in a week you don't like the job I do for you, then fire me, but at least give me a chance. That's all I ask."

And there it was, something he thought he had lost long ago, his fucking heart, and she was tugging the shit out of it. Dammit to hell. When she started to say something else, he threw up his hand and waved it away.

"Anything you hear in this office is confidential," Sloan began, but still cursed himself for not just letting her go like he knew he should. When a relieved smile beamed across her face, he knew it was going to be a damn nightmare. "Nothing you hear leaves this office."

"Yes, sir." Becky nodded, but the grin remained.

He felt something deep inside him stir at the beaming smile across her face. Jesus, he was truly fucked.

******

Sloan's silent glare quickly wiped the smile from Becky. Damn, she knew it had been a close call and that she'd better be her best if she wanted to keep the job. "Ah, would you like some coffee before I start on those files?"

"I don't drink coffee," Sloan finally said, but his glare remained.

"Oh, okay. What do you drink?" As soon as the words left her mouth, she wanted to pull them back and smack herself. He was a damn vampire. What in the hell did she think he drank? Instead of smacking herself, her hand automatically went to her throat.

His eyes followed the movement of her hand and she swore she heard him curse, but his lips didn't move though his eyes narrowed. Realizing what she'd done, Becky snapped her hand back to her side. Damn, she was an idiot.

"I don't expect that from you. I can get my own shit." His voice was gruff. "All I need you to do is find three files from this mess and then if you can file them away in alphabetical order, that will be a good start."

Becky glanced at the scattered mess next to his desk. "What files do you need?"

Sloan grabbed a pen and piece of paper, wrote down names, then handed them to her. "When you get those files just put them on my desk."

"Will do." Becky kneeled down, picked up a handful of files and took them to her small desk. "Which file cabinet do you want them in?" She hated to keep asking questions, but she didn't want to file them incorrectly.

"The one on the end is empty," Sloan replied without looking at her as he went to unlock his door.

Becky turned to get more, but Sloan was directly behind her with the rest of the files. She stepped out of his way quickly so he could place them on the floor next to her desk.

"Thank you." She smiled, but with his gaze averted, he only nodded before returning to his desk. Her eyes roamed his broad back, down to his tight ass before shooting away. "No men, no men, no men…," she chanted quietly to herself.

Chapter 4

Blaze stood back, watching the warrior trainees work on their ground fighting skills. His eyes kept going to Katrina. She was small and most of the guys there, wanting to prove their macho bullshit, just tossed her around like she was nothing. It was really starting to piss him off.

"What's got your eyes swirling?" Jared asked as he came to stand next to Blaze.

"They don't even give her a chance." Blaze nodded toward Katrina, ignoring the swirling eyes comment.

"Yeah, she's struggling." Jared frowned, his eyes narrowing when the guy she was working with bent her arm back at an odd angle, not even doing the move right. "You want to take care of that or should I?"

Blaze didn't answer when Katrina cried out. He marched over, pulling the dumbass up by the neck. "What the fuck are you trying to do, break her arm?"

"I'm fine." Katrina's voice matched her size. She was quietly spoken, but he had seen a spark in her.

Blaze ignored her, still glaring at the guy who stared wide-eyed at him. "I didn't mean to hurt her."

"You didn't." Katrina shook her head, but Blaze knew she was lying. "Come on, let's do it again."

Blaze let the guy go, his eyes going to Katrina. Instead of beating the shit out of the guy like he wanted to, he kicked off his boots. "Lie on your back," he instructed, which she did quickly. "Mount her. What's your name again?"

"John," the guy replied, his voice a little shaky.

Once John straddled Katrina, Blaze knelt. "I want you to do the arm bar again, but slowly. Get the move down before you try to speed it up. Katrina, I want you to start punching toward his face."

Katrina did without making contact.

Blaze watched as John caught her left arm. "Okay, now slowly spin and flip your right leg over her head, hugging the arm to your chest. Scoot your ass against her shoulder as tight as you possibly can as your butt hits the mat. Good. Now make sure your right leg is against her neck and your left is against her ribcage. Good." Blaze watched as John slowly took his instructions. "Lie back. The bend of her elbow should be in your crotch. Okay, good. Now arch your back, make sure her thumb is pointing toward the ceiling."

Blaze was ready to pull John's arms away if Katrina didn't tap, but once John arched, she tapped his leg with her free hand.

"Was that okay?" John asked, hope in his eyes that he'd done it right.

"It's a start and you didn't break her fucking arm off." Blaze wasn't one to give praise lightly. "Do it again."

Sitting close, Blaze watched John repeat the maneuver, but his ears picked up the snide comments about Katrina from the other trainees. He hated stupid people. There wasn't really a place in the world for dumbasses.

"Okay, Katrina." Blaze nodded at her. "Your turn."

Katrina quickly rolled to her knees then mounted John when he'd lain flat on his back.

"Guess you got to have tits to get special attention." Blaze heard the comment come from across the room.

One of the trainees snorted quietly, but not quietly enough. "John's a lucky fuck. Though if she mounted me, I'd have my dick—"

Blaze grabbed his boot and let it fly, hitting the bigmouth in the face. "Next time, motherfucker, my foot will be in that boot." Blaze knew his eyes swirled with fire, but he kept his cool… for now. "Instead of running your mouth, you should be working, because a fucking toddler could beat your ass." Blaze didn't stop glaring until the asshole was back at work, practicing with more gusto.

******

Katrina knew her face was flaming in embarrassment, but nothing anyone said in there was going to make her give up. She had nothing, absolutely nothing but this. No family, friends, nothing. She might as well be invisible other than the crude comments from the other trainees. All her life, even before she had been turned into a half-breed, she was just a passing thought to most. She was used to it; sick of it, but used to it. She wanted to make a difference. Wanted to belong. Wanted to feel important, but even when the sickness had begun to hit all the half-breeds and they'd finally received permission to be turned, she had been overlooked. It wasn't until Jill found her throwing up that she had been taken to Slade. Katrina had refused Slade to be the one who'd turn her. Jill was his mate and she'd respected Jill too much to let him do it. It had become a big ordeal. She'd been ready to leave until Blaze had stepped in.

"Katrina?" Blaze's deep voice broke her thoughts. "Ignore that shit and do the arm bar."

Katrina nodded to the Warrior who had changed her, saved her life. She worshipped him but knew the feelings weren't mutual. With that thought, she focused on her directive, knowing that nothing she could do could make a man like Blaze notice her. When she spun to flip her leg over John's head, she failed to lift her leg high enough, causing her foot to smash into John's face.

"Oh, I'm so sorry." Katrina let go of his arm, hopping off him. Blood poured from his nose. She cringed at the snickers surrounding her.

"It's okay." John held his nose, his watering eyes glancing at Blaze, who nodded for him to go to the bathroom.

She didn't even want to look at Blaze. She was worthless and it showed in every damn thing she did. But still she fought and refused to believe what her stepfather had told her more times that she could count.

"You are not fit for anything, Katrina," he would say with such hatred it burned her soul. "You are worthless."

"Hey?" Blaze's voice broke into her dark thoughts.

Without saying a word, she looked over at him. He was on his back, his stare penetrating.

"You need to focus on the present." Blaze's voice was low and deep.

Surprise that he somehow knew she was reliving a past best left forgotten, she nodded.

"Good, now mount me," Blaze ordered, his gaze daring her to do anything else.

Her stomach rose to her throat while her eyes widened as they ran down his large, hard body. No way could this be happening. Quickly looking behind her to see if John was coming back from the bathroom, she swallowed hard, seeing no sign of him.

"Today, Katrina," Blaze all but growled, growing inpatient.

Jumping, Katrina quickly straddled Blaze. He was so big compared to her that her knees barely touched the floor. How many damn times has she thought of this exact scenario, except in her scenario, he had added "baby" to his demand of "mount me." Now that she was living her thoughts of Blaze, she was scared to death she'd make a complete ass out of herself.

As Blaze raised his arms for her to do her arm bar maneuver, her mind went completely blank. All she could do was stare down into his strong, fierce face and focus on not drooling. She has no control over her body's reaction to their contact. It wasn't until she saw the understanding of her predicament in his eyes that she began to panic. No way in hell was he to know her feelings. She had to do something fast.

She punched him in the face.

"What in the fuck are you doing?" Blaze bellowed, using his arms to push himself up with her still straddling him.

"Oh, I, ah...." Katrina figured the words weren't going to come so she shrugged.

Blaze cursed a couple more times before lying back. "Katrina, do the arm bar." His eyes narrowed. "*Without* any contact to my face, that comes later. You need to get this down before you can move on."

Katrina nodded, wishing she could disappear. She knew she was being watched and laughed at, which she should be used to, but it still hurt. She had never been good at anything, and having the chance to maybe do something awesome, she instead was crushing on the man she had to count on to do that something special.

"Grab his arm." Jared knelt down beside them.

She knew this, but she was such a klutz it didn't matter if she knew it; she'd mess it up.

"They might as well just let her go," one of the guys grumbled. "She's just holding us back."

Seeing the look on Blaze's face daring her to make them see different, she grabbed his arm and in a fluid motion, had Blaze's strong muscled arm in an arm bar that would make any MMA fighter proud.

"There you go." Jared gave her a gentle slap on the back before moving on to help others.

Blaze tapped, then sat up when Katrina released his arm. "Good job." He stood and nodded to John, who was heading toward them with Kleenex stuck up his nose. "Keep working on it with that confidence and you'll be shutting up a lot of assholes in here."

Before Katrina could respond, Blaze had picked up his boot and headed toward the other one he had thrown. Not wanting him to see her staring at him, she looked away only to face John.

"I'm really sorry." She cringed, eyeing the tissue. She then grinned because John really did look funny.

"I'm sure I'll be bleeding more of my blood before this is all said and done." He chuckled. "Now come and try that again, but this time watch the nose."

Katrina laughed then mounted John, her eyes meeting Blaze's, who stood against the wall watching every move she made. Suddenly she became very worried about John's well-being, because with Blaze watching her constantly, her klutziness was going to make many appearances.

Chapter 5

Becky stored the last document with a sigh. There had been over three hundred files. The last set she'd organized were records related to deceased Warriors. She'd remembered seeing on the news about the Warriors who had been killed during a Warrior initiation not long ago. At the time, Becky had had no connection with the VC, but she'd still felt sad. After reading about the aftermath in the files, her sorrow had grown deeper.

Picking up the files Sloan had asked for, she turned to see him sitting at his desk texting on his phone. She had never seen a busier man in her life. People constantly came in the office while his phone rang and dinged nonstop. Meanwhile, she'd filed all day. Though it was her first day, she was already trying to figure out what more she could do to help him.

Jill and Caroline had invited her to lunch, but she'd waved them off and decided to work through. She had forgotten hers anyway at home in her rush not to be late. They had stayed for only a few minutes to see if she had any questions, but she really didn't have any. She worked for Sloan Murphy and if she needed questions answered, she would ask him. Like, where her scooter keys were for one.

Gathering her courage, she stood and headed toward his desk. "Here are the files you asked for."

Sloan looked up from his phone and reached out, taking them. "Thank you."

"You're welcome," she replied, hating how awkward she felt with him, but he was a very intimidating man. "Is there anything else you need me to do before I leave?"

"Actually, yes, can you find one more?" He shuffled around papers on his desk. "I need Ronan McDonald's file."

Becky made her way to the filing cabinet, pleased she remembered the name because it reminded her of Ronald McDonald, though the

Warrior's picture was far from Ronald McDonald, with a dark exotic look, not the white clown face and bright red hair. Why did all these Warriors have to be so damn good-looking?

Before she reached the cabinet, her phone rang in her back pocket. Grabbing it, she frowned when she saw her now ex-husband's number. Dammit, she really needed to talk to the asshole, but she was still on the clock. If she didn't answer, God only knew how long it would before she got hold of him. Glancing quickly over her shoulder, Becky saw that Sloan was preoccupied so she answered her phone.

"Hello," she said, trying to sound breezy. Her ex, Frank Spencer, would love nothing more than to think she was wasting away just waiting for his call. She had left the message two days ago, the jerk.

"What do you want?" Frank's voice sounded annoyed.

"I don't want anything," Becky snapped, then took a calming breath. Oh, how she hated this man. "But your son needs books and that is part of our settlement agreement and so far, you haven't done anything."

"He's eighteen, Becky," Frank snapped in her ear. "He can get a job and buy his own books. If you hadn't babied him, he would be a man by now."

"He does have a job, Frank," Becky snapped back, forgetting where she was. "And he is more of a man than his father will ever be. Now pay him the money or I will be calling my lawyer. You agreed to this and I will make sure you hold up to your end of the bargain. If not, I will take *my* house back and half *your* damn money."

"You are such a fucking bitch!" Frank screamed over the phone before he hung up on her.

"Damn straight I am, you asshole, piece-of-shit dick breath." Becky had pulled the phone away from her ear and was growling at it. Then she dropped it to her side, took a deep breath, and cranked her neck back and forth before she realized where she was. "Shit," she whispered, sensing Sloan was staring at her; she could actually feel his gaze on her back because the little hairs on her neck stood on end.

Without even looking at him, she opened the cabinet and took her time searching for the file he needed. Knowing she couldn't put off facing him much longer, she grabbed the file she'd passed over at least six times and pulled it out. Closing the drawer, she turned. Sure enough, Sloan was staring straight at her.

"Here you go." She handed it to him. "And sorry about that. It won't happen again, but I knew if I didn't answer I wouldn't be able to get hold of him again and I really needed to talk to him."

"Who, dick breath?" Sloan tilted his head. His eyes crinkled in a smile, but his lips didn't curve.

"My ex." Becky shifted from foot to foot. "Like I said, it won't happen again and I know that wasn't very professional of me, but—"

He held up his hand. "You don't need to explain to me." Sloan looked down at the file. "If you heard some of the conversations in this office, you'd understand that nothing fazes me."

"Yeah, well, it still was very unprofessional, but he makes me so mad and I'm not a very good curser when I'm mad." Becky couldn't believe she was having this conversation with her boss of one day.

"Asshole, piece-of-shit dick breath, probably would have gotten you a high five from some of the Warriors around here," Sloan teased with a cocked eyebrow.

Becky chuckled, immediately relaxing. "Well, thank you for understanding."

"No problem." He smiled and every lady part hit high alert. Sweet baby Jesus, a frowning Sloan was handsome, but a full-on smiling Sloan Murphy was what women's dreams were made of.

Dammit, his mouth was moving and she had no idea what he was saying. "I'm sorry, what?"

His eyes narrowed slightly, but he repeated himself. "Tomorrow I will set you up on the accounting."

"Thank God." Jill walked in with a relieved grin. "Love ya, boss man, but those late paychecks just aren't doing it."

"Yeah, well no paycheck could be a bitch also, so watch yourself," Sloan shot back.

"So, how did your first day go?" Jill asked, her smile beaming before she turned and frowned at Sloan. "Was he mean to you?"

"It went fine." Becky kind of felt sorry for Sloan. He seriously wasn't that bad if you didn't make him mad, and she had no plans to do that. "And no, not at all."

"Jill, get the fuck out of my office," Sloan grumbled, reaching in his drawer and pulling out Becky's scooter keys.

"He's just kidding." Jill waved him away with a smile.

"No, I'm not." Sloan growled.

Becky couldn't help but smile. Even with all their bitching back and forth, the respect they had for each other was obvious.

"Getting kicked out of the office again, Jill?" Jared asked as he walked in with Slade and Sid following.

Taking a step back from the desk, Becky watched as Slade, who was handsome as sin, put his large hand on Jill's shoulder affectionately. She felt a ping of... not jealously, but something she couldn't quite put her finger on. Loneliness maybe. Shaking the feeling away, she glanced at her keys on Sloan's desk next to his large hand and she suddenly wondered what it would feel like— *No, just stop it!*

"So what's up, boss?" Sid sat in one of the chairs and started to raise his feet, but stopped midraise when Sloan growled.

"These are my picks." Sloan gave them each a file of different Warriors. "Check them out and give me your opinion. Right now I'm only bringing in one."

"This Ronald McDonald seems like a good pick." Sid thumbed through the file.

Becky snorted with a surprised chuckle. When everyone looked at her, she cleared her throat. "Sorry." She shifted uncomfortably. Knowing she should just keep her mouth closed, she felt the need to explain. "I thought that when I saw his name. Even though he looks nothing like the McDonald's...." Jesus, why couldn't she shut the hell up?

Sid stared at her for a moment then gave her a nod before looking at Sloan. "She'll do."

"Will fit in perfectly." Jared chuckled without looking up from his file.

Becky watched Sloan roll his eyes with a head shake. Damn, she needed to be more careful. Not everyone liked her weird sense of humor. Well, except Jared and Sid, but they didn't sign her paycheck.

"Ronan would be my pick also, but I want everyone's input." Sloan ignored it all. He was all business. "The rest are out on patrol, but when they come in, I'll get their pick. If it's different from what you all feel, we'll take a vote."

"Sounds good to me." Jared put the file back on Sloan's desk. "So anything you need me to do tonight? Tessa is working so if not, I'm going to head on over to the bar and hang with her."

Sloan's eyes went to Becky. "Actually you're good to go, Jared. I need Jill and Slade." He stood, grabbing a set of keys off a board behind his desk, and handed them to her.

"Those aren't mine." Becky frowned, not taking them.

"They are as long as you work for me." Slade's tone was sharp, daring her to argue. "As long as you are working here, you will drive one of our cars."

"But—" Becky tried to argue, but Sloan just shook his head.

"Jill will follow you home on the scooter and Slade can pick her up." Sloan sat down as if it were a done deal.

"That's really not necessary." Becky was surprised that her scooter was causing such an issue.

"It is, and any more conversation on the matter is pointless," Sloan added, his eyes daring her.

It took everything Becky had not to open her mouth, but she needed this job.

"It doesn't matter what you say, he isn't budging." Jill filled the awkward silence, then caught the scooter keys that Sloan tossed her. "Sloan doesn't budge, ever."

"I can at least drive my scooter home," Becky argued.

Jill glanced at Sloan, who shook his head. "Nope, I got it."

Becky once again tried to argue, but Sloan's phone rang and he answered, the look he shot her saying he was done with the conversation. With a frown, she grabbed her bag and followed Jill and Slade out of the room.

"This is crazy." Becky huffed as soon as they were outside. "I'm a big girl. I can drive myself home. I've done it for a while now."

"Hey." Jill grinned at her. "You're in Warrior territory now. They are a little protective. Get used to it and pick your battles. Although, there will be very few battles you can win with the boss man."

"Wanna bet?" Becky said, but then realized she was getting into a car and not on her scooter.

Chapter 6

Katrina stepped out of her small shower, putting her directly in front of her sink and mirror. Wiping the fog off the mirror, she stared at her reflection and yep, she looked the same except for her matching golden eyes. The less she looked in the mirror at herself, the better. What really sucked for her was she looked the same as she did when she was turned and would stay that way forever.

Picking up a clump of her wet, flaming red hair, she frowned. It hung down her back, which regularly got in her way during training, but she couldn't bring herself to cut the frizzy mess, knowing it would never grow back. If she regretted it, it would be a regret she would have to live a lifetime with, and she already had more than enough regrets to deal with.

The only thing she had ever really liked about her appearance was gone. Her dark green eyes had always glowed brightly against the redness of her hair. Now they glowed golden, which totally clashed with her hair. With a disgusted huff, she walked out of the small bathroom into her one-room sanctuary. With a bed and dresser, it was pretty sparse.

Glancing at the door, she made sure she had locked it before walking around totally naked. Reaching for the dresser, Katrina opened one drawer and inside was her meager wardrobe. Two shirts, three pair of jeans, a week's worth of underwear, as well as the only dress she owned.

After she had been brought to the Warrior compound, Katrina had left to grab her only belongings she had stashed behind a Dollar General. She'd been sleeping there before she was arrested for being a half-breed, which seemed like forever ago. She'd had no money, nor any real skills to get a job. Life had been tough.

With a weary sigh, she grabbed the dress and put it on. Even though it was getting colder, she needed to keep her other clothes clean because jeans took forever to air dry. She had actually borrowed a pair of sweats and a T-shirt from Steve to train in, and swam in the outfit.

Once dressed, Katrina sat on her bed and stared at the door. She didn't feel sorry for herself, never had. Even though she'd been dealt a shitty hand in life more than once, she sought solutions. That was her motto: seek solutions for the shit hand you are dealt and solve it. Glancing down at her threadbare blue summer dress that hit the floor, she shrugged, then glanced at her tennis shoes, deciding to go barefoot. Problem solved.

Standing, she straightened her shoulders. She was hungry and it was time to face whatever was to come once she left her little sanctuary. She didn't know why she should be nervous; she was pretty much invisible to everyone anyway, and she liked it that way. She could observe, which she did very well, and she knew that not everyone ignored her on purpose. They were very busy people, that was all.

Reaching the door, she jumped when someone knocked from the other side.

"Hey, Katrina," Steve's voice called out. "You in there?"

Katrina opened the door and smiled. She really liked Steve; he made her laugh. "Hi."

"Hello," he answered with a hesitant frown. "Can I talk to you for a minute?"

"Sure." Katrina stepped aside, letting him in. "When did you get back?" She knew he had gone to Kentucky for a job and he had been so excited. She hoped it had gone well for him, but the way he was acting, she was afraid it hadn't.

"Ah, a while ago," he replied as he started pacing in her small room. It only took him three steps before he turned and paced three steps the other way.

"Are you okay?" She wasn't used to seeing Steve agitated.

"Yes and no." His eyes shifted nervously to her and then away. He paced twice more, then stopped. "I found someone."

"Oh, did you go to Kentucky to find someone?" Katrina wasn't sure she was following, since she really didn't know the reason he had been sent to Kentucky.

Steve looked at her, puzzled. "No." Then he grabbed her by the arms and sat her on the bed. "Listen, I don't want to hurt you, but you need to know."

"Um, all right." Katrina frowned, wondering what in the world was going on.

Steve cursed and shook his head before squeezing his eyes shut. "Her name is Leda." His eyes popped open to see her reaction and she was sure what he saw was total confusion. "I think I'm in love with her. I'm sorry, Katrina."

Katrina's eyes popped open wide. "Oh!"

"Damn. I didn't mean for it to happen, but it did." Steve sat next to her, his lower lip puckered in a pout.

Smiling, Katarina put her hand on his. "Steve, it's okay. I'm happy for you." She laughed at the relief that crossed his face.

"I didn't break your heart?" Steve searched her face.

"No, you didn't break my heart, and Leda is a very lucky girl," Katrina reassured him. Steve was so sweet and funny, but totally not her type. She didn't tell him that. She had no clue where he'd got the idea she would be heartbroken. Though Steve was who she had the most contact with, she didn't have that type of feelings for him and found herself relieved he had found someone.

"Oh, thank God." Steve fell back on the bed in a dramatic fashion.

"Well, do you have a picture of Leda?" Katrina laughed at his reaction.

"Of course I do." He snorted then sat up straight before tilting to remove the phone out of his back pocket. He handed her his phone after he pulled up the picture. "Isn't she a fox?"

Katrina stared at the picture of the beautiful girl and smiled. "She is gorgeous."

"Well actually, she's a wolf." Steve took his phone back and stared at it. "A foxy wolf." He laughed at his own words.

"Did you meet her while you were in Kentucky?" Katrina sighed happily. It felt good to hold a conversation with someone.

"Yeah, and almost lost my life in the process. The alpha is her guardian and damn near killed me when he found us kissing." Steve's eyes widened, then narrowed badass style, at least badass style for Steve. "But I showed him what was up."

Katrina chuckled, then cleared her throat. "I bet you did."

Steve nodded and glanced at the picture one more time before returning it to his pocket. "So, now that's out of the way, what are you up to?"

"Thinking of going to get something to eat." Katrina stood then held out her hand. "Care to join me?"

"Hells yeah." Steve took her hand and opened the door. "You're pretty awesome, Katrina."

"You're not too bad yourself, Steve." She let him lead her down the hall, around the corner and down another hall to the kitchen.

******

Blaze sat in the kitchen eating a bowl of the chili Sid had simmering on the stove. The guy was goofy as hell, but the fucker could cook and made one hell of a Warrior. He was pretty content at the compound, more so than anywhere else he had been. Steady work, steady good pay, and steady friendships, but not too close. The team did their thing and he did his, just the way he liked it. He did not consider himself a Warrior, though. He *wasn't* a Warrior, but Sloan treated him as if he was and as long as he was pulling a paycheck and could leave anytime he wanted, he was fine with that. No ties, just the way he liked it and the only way shit worked for him.

Looking up, he watched Steve and Katrina come into the kitchen hand in hand. His first initial reaction was to punch the kid in the face, but he stomped that feeling down quickly. He had no rights to Katrina. None. He had changed her, that was all. His feelings were normal after changing someone. There was also that bond between the two people. It didn't matter if it were a man or woman. He was more or less her maker.

"Oh, hey, Blaze." Steve noticed him. "How's the chili?"

Blaze let his eyes leave Katrina and go to Steve. "Not bad," was his only answer.

Katrina said nothing and barely looked at him. He knew she had feelings for him; he sensed it. Another reason he had to be careful as nothing could come of her feelings. He was there to support her training and that was it, nothing more. His eyes roamed her body in the faded thin summer dress that dropped to the hem, and he knew she wore no shoes.

"Yeah, Sid can pretty much cook the shit out of anything." Steve walked over with a huge bowl. "And his chili has a definite kick to it. I bet spicy food doesn't bother you."

"The hotter the better," Blaze replied with a half grin. It was hard not to like Steve. He had no filter and said whatever came to his mind. He was actually surprised he had lived this long around the Warriors, but he knew any one of them would die for the kid.

Katrina sat quietly eating her chili, gently blowing on each spoonful before putting it in her mouth. Blaze shifted in his seat. He needed to stop watching her do that shit. As the kitchen started to fill with everyone coming in to eat, he watched Katrina sink deeper into herself and try to fade so not to be noticed.

Duncan and Pam walked in with Daniel, who went straight to Katrina. She pushed her food away and her full focus was on the little boy while letting Duncan and Pam eat. Conversation went on around him, but he watched only her. She was different than anyone he had ever known. Her heart was wide open and she silently screamed for affection. It seemed he was the only one who heard.

Standing up quickly as if that would quiet his mind, he walked over to clean his bowl and put it away. Without saying a word to anyone, he headed out of the kitchen. Caroline was heading his way when he stopped her.

"How you doing, Blaze?" Caroline smiled up at him. At least she wasn't looking behind him at the dead people she said followed him around. That was the main reason he avoided her and her sister. He needed no reminders of his past; the reminders lived in his memory.

"Good, and you?" Blaze responded politely as he pulled out his wallet.

"Can't complain," she replied, then took a big whiff of air. "Ready for some of Sid's famous chili. Been smelling it all day."

"Just finished off a bowl and it's as good as it smells. He's a pain in my ass, but can't complain about his cooking." He grinned, pulling hundreds out of his wallet.

"He's a pain in everyone's ass." She chuckled, her eyes going from his to the money he held.

"Can you do me a favor?" Blaze hated to ask anything of anyone, but this was something he couldn't do himself.

"Sure." Caroline nodded, her eyes curious.

"From what I can tell, Katrina has only a few changes of clothes and she has been wearing a pair of Steve's old sweats and T-shirt for her training." Blaze handed her the money. "Could you see she gets what she needs?"

"Of course." Caroline frowned. "I feel so bad. We should have known that she needed things, but she never said anything."

Blaze knew Katrina wouldn't say anything. She had become sick before anyone even noticed she hadn't been changed to a full blood, him included. "If you need more money, let me know."

"You're a true gentleman, Blaze." Caroline smiled, touching his arm, then quickly removed her hand.

He laughed at that. If she only knew. "No, just making sure one of the trainees has what they need to focus on their training. Nothing more, nothing less."

"Should I tell her where this came from?" she called out as he walked away.

He didn't answer because he didn't really care. He was doing what he had just told Caroline, making sure all trainees had a fair shot. At least that was what he was telling himself.

Chapter 7

After showering, Becky headed toward her refrigerator. She was starved and her stomach was growling loudly. Seeing nothing but a half-eaten salad, a piece of three-day-old pizza, two beers, three bottles of water, and a container she was afraid to open, she closed the door. Opening the cabinet next to the fridge, she frowned when faced with the peanut butter. She was sick to death of the spread, plus she had no crackers, bread, or jelly. A spoonful of peanut butter was not doing it for her.

Glancing at the clock, she knew she had time to head out for a quick bite, but didn't know if she had enough money. She frowned, thinking about the car sitting in front of her house. She was going to have to gas it up soon, since it was only on a quarter of a tank. That was the thing she loved about her scooter, it was cheap, and cheap was all she could afford.

Searching around, she finally found enough extra change to buy dinner. What she really wanted was a Corner Street hamburger, but the bar food catty-corner from her small rental home was expensive. Yep, a White Castle slider with a side of onion chips was going to have to do. Reaching for her keys, she stopped to stare at the two sets. Picking up her scooter keys, she headed toward the door. She had a while before her first paycheck and she was scrounging for change for a slider. If she was going to have to gas up the car, she'd just use it for work and nothing else.

Even though she struggled financially, her son had always been taken care of and she was good with what she had. She would struggle before she ever counted on a man for anything ever again. It was taking a while, but she would get back on her feet. Her divorce had been nasty, her ex-husband cruel, and she was finally free of him, other than the link to their son.

She had gotten pregnant at sixteen. Frank had, more or less, stuck around until Frankie Jr. was eight. For two years she had been the mother, father, breadwinner, problem solver, and whatever else came with being a single parent. She'd never really loved Frank, sad to say, and made a huge mistake by having unprotected sex, especially at such a young age, with a boy she didn't really love.

Frank showed back up in their lives two years after disappearing. To this day, she didn't know why she'd taken him back, but she had and even married him after a few more years. Looking back, she knew it was from desperation of wanting help. Having a man she didn't really love to shoulder some of the responsibility was better than nothing, so she'd settled. At thirty-four years old, with her life pretty much passing her by, the only worthy thing she had done was raise a decent kid who she loved more than anything.

But she was ready to change that. She wanted to go back to school—for what, she hadn't figured out—but she wanted something more out of life. Frankie was good. He was in college and needed little help, which she fought tooth and nail to help him, and he was also a man. The hard part was over. She finally had a decent-paying job. It would just take a few paychecks to get ahead, but she could see some light at the end of the long, dark tunnel she had been clawing through. Frankie had a steady job, had won a few scholarships, and had been approved for student loans.

Once on the road, she put all that in the back of her mind as she took her time enjoying the cool night. She loved September weather in the Tristate. Warm days and cool nights. Fall was her favorite time of year. She hated winter, but summer was okay. She would have loved the summer months if it didn't get so humid.

She could see the White Castle sign and the place didn't look too crowded, which was a relief. She wanted to eat, then get home and go to bed. Puttering into the parking lot, she parked and climbed off the scooter, pocketing her keys. Walking in, she did a quick glance around. Newport, Kentucky, used to be known for its high crime, but since they had built the aquarium and the Newport Levee was bustling with new business, Newport had a new face and she enjoyed the atmosphere. Of course there were bad areas, but every community had its issues.

Walking inside, she stared straight toward the counter, not wanting to make eye contact with anyone. She was a woman alone, at night, with a scooter for escape. She wasn't stupid; she knew she had to be aware. She'd taken a few self-defense courses and could put a hurtin' on a pair of balls with a well-placed kick if she had to.

"Can I help you?" the server behind the counter asked, sounding as if he hated his life.

"Two sliders with cheese, a small onion chip, and small tea." Becky pulled the money out of her pocket. She knew the total by heart and laid it on the counter. Seeing the look on the guy's face, she frowned, embarrassed. "Sorry about the change."

He didn't say anything, but counted it, put it in the register, and printed out her receipt. While waiting for her food, she went to the condiment station and grabbed some napkins, a straw, and ketchup. By the time she finished and returned to the counter, her sad little meal sat cooling on a blue tray, the counter guy nowhere to be seen. Grabbing her food, Becky headed for an empty table and sat, still not making eye contact with anyone.

She finally let her eyes wander halfway through her meal. An older woman sat alone slowly eating. Every once in a while, the woman would look out the window and just stare. Becky felt her loneliness. Looking down at her own food, it started to blur. A sudden sense of her own loneliness hit her hard. Was she going to be just like that poor old woman sitting alone in a White Castle on a Monday night? Who was she kidding? She was that old woman sitting alone at a White Castle on a Monday night.

Looking back up, her eyes met those of the woman, an understanding in her old, clouded eyes. She gave Becky a sad smile. Feeling the walls closing in on her, Becky quickly cleaned up her mess and stood. Dumping her half-eaten food in the garbage, her eyes once again met the woman's. Becky gave her a nod and a small smile, so not to be rude, and headed out the door.

Straddling her scooter, she stared out into the night. She didn't want to go home. Angrily wiping a tear from her cheek, she started her scooter and headed for the river, hoping to outrun her loneliness and sad little life.

******

Sloan sat on his bike hidden by darkness. He had been doing a run and happened to see a bright pink scooter parked at White Castle. He had circled and seen through the window Becky sitting alone, eating.

Even as angry as he was that she was out at night, alone and still riding that damn deathmobile, he had to grin with a shake of his head. They did a lot of patrolling in the area because activity was high, especially near the river around the Levee. Never once had he seen her bright pink scooter, and he definitely would have remembered if he had. What were the fucking odds?

His eyes scanned the area. Things seemed quiet, but that could change in a heartbeat. Checking his phone, he sent a text letting Duncan know he would be late for their meeting and to go ahead without him. Straddling his bike, his arms crossed over his chest, he sat alert to his surroundings as he stared at Becky, his secretary, and he felt responsible for her safety… already. Fuck!

Starting his bike when he saw her stand, he watched as she quickly got on her scooter and started it up—still without a helmet. He growled with a frown. She wiped her cheek, then stared into the darkness before taking off. Glancing back inside to see who in the hell could have made her cry, he saw only an old woman staring out the window.

Sloan pulled out, staying far enough behind her not to be noticed, and followed. He wanted to make sure she made it home safely before continuing with his night. Though, she was going in the wrong direction. He knew the street she lived on because of the extensive background check on her, and he knew these streets well. Seeing her signal turn on, he knew exactly where she was going, and it puzzled him. Why in the hell would she be going to the river?

Slowing down, he waited until she turned before he accelerated and made the turn himself. By the time he rounded the corner onto Riverboat Row, she was already off her scooter and walking toward the riverbank where benches sat. Pulling into a space near one of the many restaurants, he searched the area for danger. Once again he sat on his bike and watched.

As time passed, he wondered what the hell was wrong with him. He had shit to do, but there he was watching a woman he barely knew, and he didn't want to leave. Jesus, wouldn't the guys have a field fucking day with this. A movement up the bank drew his attention. In one fluid motion, he was off his bike but didn't take a step.

A man stood next to the trees watching Becky as well as checking out his surroundings. He hadn't spotted Sloan yet, but Sloan blended into the darkness well.

"Move along, motherfucker," Sloan said under his breath, his eyes narrowing on the guy. The guy obviously felt confident he was alone, except for Becky, and he made his move. So did Sloan. "Shit!"

Sloan made it to Becky before the asshole could. It took a minute for the guy, who had obviously been drinking, to realize Sloan had appeared. He stumbled to a stop.

He sized Sloan up and by the look on his face, he knew he might be in a trouble. "Oh, hey." The guy frowned, then tried to look around Sloan, who had blocked Becky with his body. "I was just seeing if the lady needed help."

Hearing Becky stand behind him, Sloan turned his head slightly to make sure she was still blocked and out of any danger. His eyes went back to the man. "No help needed." Sloan's voice was deep and stern.

Whether it was a booze or just plain stupidity, the guy didn't turn to leave. He continued to stand his ground and opened his mouth. "Well, I'd like to hear it from her because maybe she needs help from you." His statement came out cocky and his hands fisting told Sloan he was about to deliver an ass whopping this guy would never forget.

Sloan's smile was vicious. He looked at the ground for a second, then back up, tilting his head. "Do you really want to do this?" His tone offered a clear warning. "Because I can tell you right now, you will lose."

The man reached behind him and pulled out a knife. "Oh, you think so?" The man waved the knife around, tossing it from hand to hand. "I think not, asshole."

"Becky, stay behind me," Sloan ordered, his eyes never leaving the dumbass threatening him.

"Yeah, Becky," the man snarled. "Don't go far because after I'm done with hero here, me and you have some business of our own." He crudely humped his pelvis.

Knowing the man had to take a step toward him to use the knife, Sloan waited patiently. He emptied his mind as he watched the prick showboat. Unless that knife was made of silver, it wouldn't do shit to him. It would hurt like a bitch, but that was it. The bad thing for this asshole, or any asshole who came at Sloan, was that he used pain as his motivation to win.

"Be careful." He heard Becky's whispered words behind him, but didn't respond.

"Well, are you going to use that thing or play with it all night?" Sloan finally grew tired of waiting for the idiot to make his move.

Sloan's question slowed the man's showboating down at little as he hesitated. "Hey, I'm in charge here," the man slurred, his eyes narrowing.

"Yeah, well, fuck that." Sloan had the man by the throat and the knife out of his hand before the asshole could blink. "You plan on using that knife on the lady?"

The man's eyes bugged out of his head from lack of air. He tried to sputter some words, but Sloan squeezed his throat too tightly.

Sloan pulled out his phone and made a call. "Need you down at Riverboat Row by the Beer Sellar." He put his phone back in his pocket before looking back at the guy. "Not much of a badass now, are you?"

The man finally passed out and went limp. Tossing him to the ground, Sloan then turned to look at Becky. Wide-eyed, she stared at the unconscious man.

"Did you kill him?" she whispered.

"Not yet," Sloan replied, his eyes narrowed in anger. "And if Duncan doesn't get here before the bastard wakes up, I make no promises."

Chapter 8

One minute Becky was reflecting on life as she stared at the river and the next she was watching Sloan grab a knife-wielding man by the throat. Where in the hell had he come from? She had checked out the area before climbing off her scooter and heading down to the bench she always sat at, and saw no one.

Without Sloan saying a word, she knew he was pissed and not just at the knocked-out man.

"What in the hell are you doing out here this time of night, alone?" Sloan's voice was stern, as if he were talking to a child.

"I, ah…." Becky was a little taken back by his anger toward her and actually, she didn't appreciate being talked to that way.

He didn't let her continue. "Why are you riding that damn deathmobile? Where is the fucking car?"

"It's, ah…." Becky tried again, her anger boiling close to the surface.

"And why are you not wearing a helmet?" He continued down a list of things he was obviously pissed about.

She started to open her mouth, then shut it to make sure he was finished. He wasn't.

"Do you have any idea what could have happened to you if I hadn't been here?" Sloan got louder with each question he asked, but he wouldn't shut up long enough for her to answer. When she just stood there staring at him, he threw up his hands. "Well?"

"Are you finished?" Becky put her hands on her hips.

Sloan glared at her for a second. "Yes, I am."

"What are you doing here?" Becky asked, glaring back at him.

"I'm the one asking the questions!" he bellowed. When the man made a noise, Sloan put his large foot on the guy's chest without even looking; he was too busy scowling at her.

"I answer to you between the hours of seven and four, Mr. Murphy." She huffed, then turned to leave, but stopped and turned around to look at him. "I don't know what I did to make you so angry at me, but thank you for well, you know." She waved her hand toward the guy on the ground.

Becky walked away, realizing her shitty night just got shittier and had taken a nosedive straight to hell. So much for getting back on her feet. She probably didn't have a job anymore, but seriously, did he have to get all crazy and start questioning her decisions like that? Hurrying to her scooter, she hopped on and took off, barely missing a car that was passing.

By the time she arrived home, she felt awful because honestly, everything Sloan had yelled about was for her safety. And how did she repay him? By acting like an ungrateful shrew. She knew why. Her ex-husband had always made her feel stupid, and she had felt Sloan's questions were an attack against her judgment, which in turn made her feel as if she wasn't smart enough to make good decisions. Having time to cool off and think about it, she begrudgingly admitted to herself he was right.

Before she could climb off her scooter, a motorcycle sped down the road and pulled in behind her. Sloan sat staring at her for a few seconds before turning off his engine.

"Do you even know how close you were to hitting Duncan?" Sloan asked, his voice a little calmer.

"How do you know where I live?" She stared at him wide eyes.

Sloan closed his eyes for a second and cursed under his breath.

"Background check." He opened his eyes, pinning her to the spot. "Now answer my question."

"Which one?" she replied, then sighed. "I was hungry and didn't have anything here to eat. I drove my scooter because it's cheaper on gas. I forgot my helmet again, but I was only planning on going up the street, and I wasn't that close to Duncan's car." There, she'd answered every question he had asked. Maybe he wouldn't fire her.

"You forgot to answer one." He crossed his arms over his chest, no longer glaring.

Becky thought for a minute. "No, I don't think I did." She tilted her head. The music from the bar across from her house drifted toward them. She couldn't believe he'd followed her from the river. He was most likely there to fire her officially and save himself the trouble when she showed up to work the next day.

"It's actually the most important question I asked," Sloan replied, then glanced across the street to the bar when a few people exited the establishment loudly. His attention swung back to her and he waited for a few more intense seconds for her to answer. "Do you have any idea what could have happened to you if I hadn't been there?"

She started to ask him why exactly had he been there, but remembered he didn't seem to like when she answered his questions with a question of her own. Then again, she really wanted to know, so decided to live on the edge.

"And why exactly were you there?" She waited for him to blow up again.

"Are you trying to make me angry?" His voice wasn't angry really, just more curious than anything else.

"Am I fired?" shot out of her mouth. She couldn't help it; she needed to know.

Sloan opened his mouth to say something, but then closed it and just stared at her. Finally, he shook his head and chuckled. "No, Becky. You're not fired."

"Ah, thank God." Becky released a big sigh of relief.

"Unless…," Sloan added.

Her eyes popped open wide. "Unless what?" *Oh, crap.* She wondered what the terms would be and if she could follow them.

"You stop answering my questions with questions." He cocked an eyebrow at her, but no chuckle followed his statement.

"I'll do my best," Becky hedged, not wanting to promise something she may totally fail at. "Listen, sometimes I get a little heated. I blame the red hair for that, and well, I'm sorry. And thank you for what you did. I do know what could have happened if you hadn't been there. I go to that same spot all the time and never has anything happened to me."

"You shouldn't be out alone in a secluded area this late at night," Sloan warned her, his voice stern.

"You're right and usually it's not this late. I just wasn't ready to come back home." She shrugged, looking away from him. "Haven't you ever just done something on a whim?"

"No." Sloan's one-word reply said it all.

"Oh." She glanced up at him, then back to her dark house that she didn't want to walk into alone. Her independent self cursed her for being an idiot, but her lonely self patted her on the shoulder. "Would you like to come in for a minute? I have two beers as an offering of thanks."

She waited for his answer. Half of her wanted him to say no, the other half begged for him to say yes. What in the hell was wrong with her?

Didn't she just have a conversation this morning with her whole self... no men? When he didn't reply and looked from her house to her, she wished she had never asked. She felt like an idiot.

"It's not a big deal." Becky gave him a small smile. "I'm sure you have things to do. Thanks again for what you did." She started to turn toward her house, but his words stopped her.

"I could use a beer."

******

As Sloan stood in the small living room watching Becky getting him a beer, he cursed himself. What in the fuck was he doing? It was as if his mouth had a fucking mind of its own. "I could use a beer?" What in the hell was that and where in the fuck did it come from?

"Here you go." Becky handed him a Busch beer, which he must have glared at. "Sorry, I know it's not a Budw—"

"It's fine." He took a drink, doing his best not to make the famous bitter beer face. It tasted like cold piss. "Thank you."

"So what are you doing on this side of the river?" Becky asked, sitting down on her couch with a bottle of water.

Sloan leaned against the wall, holding his piss beer. "This is one of the areas we patrol" was his only explanation. He didn't know the meaning of the words small talk.

"Oh, what do you patrol for?" Becky asked, then took a drink of water.

"Bad guys." He grinned at her disappointed frown. She'd wanted juicy details, but he wasn't going to give them to her.

"You don't like to talk much, do you?" Becky finally said after a moment of awkward silence.

"No, I don't." Sloan decided to finish off his beer before it got warm. In all honesty, if it tasted like cold piss already, he was afraid of what it might taste like warm. In one long swallow, he finished it off. Becky stood to take the empty bottle.

"You want another one?" Becky tossed the empty bottle in the trash.

"I'm good, thanks." Sloan cringed at the thought of drinking another one. He had noticed how empty her refrigerator was when she had retrieved his beer, and her place was a shithole, but he also knew this area and her rent probably wasn't cheap. He pulled out his wallet, grabbed some bills, and placed them on her table.

Becky had turned to see him do it. "What is that?" She frowned when Sloan remained silent. "Listen, I don't take handouts. I may live in a shithole…"

Sloan grinned at her words that described exactly what he thought of her rental house.

"…and be low on food, but I make do."

"It's not a handout." Sloan refused to take the money back that she kept pushing at him. He watched as she looked down at his jeans pocket, then looked into his eyes. He knew his expression was daring her to try to shove the money in his pocket. "It's a pay advance, and believe me, you will earn every penny."

"A pay advance?" Becky's voice changed as she looked at the money. "Are you sure?"

"I do nothing I'm not sure about," Sloan replied, knowing that was a fucking lie. He sure didn't know why he was standing inside his secretary's house. It was time to get the hell out of there. He nodded and headed toward the door. "Thanks for the beer."

"You're welcome." Becky followed him. "Thank you for everything. I really mean it. I know I went a little nutso—again, blame it on the hair

—but I do appreciate what you've done and for the job. I promise you won't be sorry."

Sloan walked out the door and to his bike. He threw his hand up, not looking back at her. His eyes once again went to the bar. The locks on her doors needed to be replaced. A strong wind could break them. Climbing onto his bike, he fought not to look back at her, but his eyes won the battle. His eyes met hers as she stood in the doorway and gave him a wave. Rolling his bike backwards, he finally looked away as he took off down her street, her words of "I promise you won't be sorry" following him. He had a feeling he was going to be very fucking sorry.

Chapter 9

Katrina hurried to the warehouse, knowing she was going to be late. Caroline had come to her room and told her that she was taking her shopping for some clothes. At first Katrina had balked because she knew she didn't have any money, but shopping sounded too good. Caroline had told her that the Council was taking care of the costs. Katrina didn't question it. She needed not only clothes, but toothpaste and deodorant. She didn't know if, being a vampire, she needed those things, but it made her feel human again. No one ever said she stunk, but she really didn't want to be the stinky girl.

After they'd shopped all morning, they had lunch and then Caroline surprised her with a salon visit. Katrina almost told them to cut it all off, but Caroline put up a fight. So instead, they added some highlights to tone down her fire-red hair, and gave it a trim. Caroline had orchestrated it all.

The parking lot was full and with a worried frown, she hurried inside, dropped her bag, and headed out on the floor.

"Five more laps because Katrina finally decided to join us!" Jax yelled out, his eyes narrowed on Katrina.

"Sorry," Katrina huffed as she ran through the obstacles. They didn't just do laps. They had to drop, crawl, jump, roll, and anything else the warriors felt they needed to add to the course.

"Way to go, Katrina," Ben sneered at her. He was regularly on her case.

Katrina ignored him as she ran through the obstacle course, trying her best to focus, but she spotted Blaze staring at her just as she was going under the metal pipe. She hit her forehead hard, knocking her on her ass. Three guys then plowed into her.

"Come on, dammit!" another trainee hissed. "First you're late and we suffer for it and now you can't even go under a fucking pipe. Give it up, *girl*." The way he said girl was not a compliment.

Each one of them pushed off her as they stood to pass. Pushing herself up, she glared at them as she continued the course. She would not let them ruin her day.

"Get a partner," Jax ordered, and everyone hurried. The only person left was poor John.

"It's okay," John said, then grinned. "Just watch the nose."

Katrina laughed with a nod. She turned her attention to Jax, keeping her eyes focused on him and not Blaze. That was, until Jax called Blaze over.

"There are many pressure points in the body," Jax said as he started to demonstrate on Blaze.

"But we're vampires. That shit doesn't work on us," Ben said, his arms crossed arrogantly.

Before anyone could react, Blaze pinched Ben between the shoulder and neck with two fingers. "Wrong," Blaze said as Ben dropped to his knees in pain. "I'm not even applying a lot of pressure, but I can have this asshole doing anything I want by just applying a little pressure."

Katrina did her best not to smile at Ben's unpleasant situation. Actually, she was plain enjoying watching him on his knees with his eyes squeezed tightly in pain.

"Stand up," Blaze ordered. Ben followed every order until he was released. "Anyone, any size, can use pressure points to get the results you want." Blaze looked at her for a split second.

Watching as Blaze and Jax demonstrated some of the pressure points, Katrina tried not to smile or show her excitement. Finally, it was something she might be able to do well. After the demonstration, everyone paired off with their partners.

After about a half an hour of working, Katrina felt confident she had it. She even had John on the ground with his arms spread apart with just two of her fingers. It was awesome and she couldn't stop smiling.

"You're pretty damn good at this." John laughed, rubbing his shoulder. "That shit hurts."

"You want to go again or do you think you have it?" Katrina even sounded more confident. Yeah, it was a good day.

"Guess she would be good at it. I'm sure she's been getting private lessons." Ben snickered, but his glare was evil and directed at her.

"Ignore him," John said, wiping sweat from his face. "I'm good with the pressure points if you are."

"What did he mean, private lessons?" Katrina frowned, looking up at John. "I'm not getting private lessons."

John sighed. "It's just a bunch of the guys are talking about how you are staying at the VC compound while the rest of us have to find our own lodgings." John shrugged. "It's just talk, Katrina. I know you're not doing anything with the Warriors to get special treatment."

Katrina gasped in shock, her head snapping back. "That's what they're saying?"

"That's exactly what we're saying," Ben butted in. A grin curved his lips. "And while we're at it, how many of the Warriors did you have to do for your new clothes? And I bet you had to use that mouth some for the new hair."

To say she was shocked was an understatement. Her eyes roamed every trainee in the room. They all stared at her. She had been judged and found guilty of everything Ben had been saying about her, apparently. Anger, so deep, filled her to the point she was a little scared because she started to shake. She always kept her cool and was rarely angry. Even when she should get angry, she'd always take a deep breath and walk on.

In three strides she was in front of Ben, her breathing harsh. Staring into his condescending eyes, she let go and kicked him right between the legs with her shin. Once he hit the ground, she leaned down into his face while he held his balls.

"When pressure points just won't do," Katrina spat with a hiss. "Asshole."

When she stood straight up, everyone was looking at her, even Jax and Blaze. Not wanting to answer questions, she turned, walked off the floor, grabbed her bag, and headed out of the warehouse.

Katrina ran all the way back to the compound and headed straight to the kitchen, hoping to find Caroline. She needed answers. The kitchen was empty so she grabbed her phone supplied to her by the Warriors. Finding Caroline's number, she hit Call and put the phone to her ear.

"Hello," Caroline answered on the third ring.

"Hi, it's Katrina." Katrina had been wondering if any of the other trainees received a phone also. "Did all the trainees get money for clothes?"

The line was silent, effectively answering her question.

"Katrina, Blaze was only trying to help—" Caroline started, but Katrina cut her short and hung up. She was totally mortified. All the trainees thought she was whoring her way through the program. How could she face any of them again?

Running to her room, she slammed the door shut. Quickly taking off her new workout clothes, she tossed the phone on the bed. In record time she was dressed in her old jeans and a T-shirt. Folding the new clothes, she placed them on the bed. Grabbing a plastic bag, she tossed the rest of her stuff in, leaving everything else behind. With one look around, she closed the door behind her and headed for the back entrance of the compound.

The closer she got to her destination, the more she felt she was going to lose it. Her chin trembled, but she controlled it. Suddenly the skies opened up and rain poured, drenching her, yet she kept going. She didn't even try to find shelter. What did it matter, anyway? She was back to where she had been before meeting Jill. She should have known it was too good to be true, that it wouldn't last. It never did, not for her.

Seeing her destination, she looked both ways then crossed the street. It was getting late so she knew the store was closed. Crossing the parking lot, she felt the hot boil of nausea hit her. Turning the corner to the back of the Dollar Store, she was relieved that she was alone and let a tear escape.

Instead of finding somewhere to get out of the rain, Katrina tossed her bag down, leaned against the wall, and slid down. She stared out into nothing, numb to everything. Her blood tears were washed away by the cold rain. Hearing a noise to her right made her smile sadly.

"I'm back, Buck." Rolling her head, she stared at the huge ten-point buck that had come out of the woods behind the store. He gave a low snort, coming closer. "I missed you also, my friend."

As the tears continued to fall, the buck lowered himself in front of her, his legs folding underneath him. Soon other creatures came out of the woods to give comfort to Katrina, and she accepted them with open arms.

******

Blaze watched Katrina walk out of the warehouse. He gave a nod to John, who was grinning at a moaning Ben who still held his balls.

"What was that about?" Blaze nodded toward Ben. Jax had walked up also.

John looked a little uncomfortable as he glanced at the other trainees, who were watching.

"If you don't tell me, then I will beat the hell out of every motherfucker in this room until I get the answer," Blaze warned, eyeing each trainee before looking back at John. "So either tell me now and save your fellow trainees from an ass kicking, or be the most hated asshole in here by keeping quiet. Which is it going to be?"

John gulped. "Not much of a choice."

Blaze growled, grabbing the closest trainee to him, pulling his fist back.

"Okay. Okay!" John put his hands up. "There's been talk. They think Katrina has been getting special attention because she's been—"

"Been what?" Blaze growled, his anger barely in check.

"You know." John looked away from Blaze, clearly uncomfortable to even speaking the words. "Putting out for the Warriors."

Blaze looked down at Ben, who stared up at him. Walking over, he picked him up by the hair. "Is he the one spreading this shit?"

No one said a word, but Blaze knew. "I'm going to say this one time: if I hear another word against Katrina, who is one of you, I will make damn sure you never get Warrior status through here or anywhere else."

"Yes, sir," they all replied, except for Ben who looked too scared to say anything as he stared into Blaze's odd eyes.

"As for you." Blaze let go of his hair and punched him in the face. "That's what assholes get for talking about a woman like that. Warriors respect women, especially a teammate."

Ben wiped his mouth, but nodded. "I'm s-sorry," he stuttered.

"Not good enough." Blaze hissed as he passed him. "Not even close."

"Go ahead." Jax nodded at Blaze. "I got it from here."

Blaze had to make himself walk out of the warehouse before he set the whole fucking place on fire. His anger was intense, swirling around him, threatening to spiral and release. It had only been this bad once before, and that had been tragic. Focusing on the present, he climbed on his bike and headed to the compound. During the short ride, he knew he wasn't going to find Katrina.

Once there, he went inside and headed straight for her room. Knocking twice, he tried the knob. The door opened. He walked in and in one sweep, he knew he had been right. She was gone and the cell phone she had been given lay on the bed.

Heading to the Intel room, he went to the monitors. Sitting down, he played the cameras back. He stopped the rewind when he saw Katrina rushing into the compound. Blaze glanced at the time on the tape and then his watch, marking the time. Again he played them back and found the one of her leaving. Once again he marked the time. Pausing, he noted that she was carrying a yellow bag and he knew it held her belongings. She had packed up and left. Glancing at the time, he figured she'd been gone a little over a half an hour.

"Fuck!" He slammed his hand on the table, then stood and headed out the door. He should have paid more attention to what was going on with the trainees. They were all his responsibility. He would be doing the same thing for any of the other trainees. That was what he told himself, anyway, but he knew it was a lie. Climbing on his motorcycle, Blaze took off, rain pounding him as he went in search.

Chapter 10

Becky sat at her desk with Sloan leaning over her. Dammit, she had to focus. Why did he have to smell so good? Her eyes left the computer screen to lock on his large masculine hand moving her mouse around.

"This program is pretty easy to understand." His voice boomed next to her ear, making her jump. Her eyes returned to the screen so fast it made her dizzy.

Easy, she thought, *if I paid attention*. She snorted to herself, wondering what happened to her big plan of no men. She could see his reflection in the screen and saw he was staring at her.

"You think you got it?" he asked, letting go of the mouse and standing straight.

"I think so." She nodded, not sure if she were being truthful.

"Go ahead and do Adam's," Sloan instructed as he stepped back to watch. "He's less likely to kill you if his paycheck is wrong."

"What?" Becky spun in her chair to look up at him with wide eyes.

"The guys get pretty cranky when their paychecks are wrong." Sloan cocked his eyebrow. "Jill's the worst, actually."

"You're kidding, right?" Becky was freaking out now. Shit, she should have paid more attention to the program than his damn hand on her mouse. Okay, that sounded a little dirty.

"I'd protect you the first couple of times, but after that, you'd be on your own." Sloan's voice was even, his face serious… until he winked at her.

Okay, her no-man thing just went out of the window. With just a wink her insides felt on fire as they dipped, flipped, and did all sorts of shit.

She was ready to melt off her roller chair into messy goo at his feet. How in the hell was she supposed to keep her sanity with winking going on? No man ever in her life had her questioning her own sanity with just a wink.

"Becky." Sloan's voice broke into her crazy thoughts.

"Yeah?" she responded, then jumped. "Yeah! Okay, Adam."

Turning toward the screen, knowing her face was blotched red with embarrassment, she grabbed the mouse, still warm from his touch, and sighed. *Holy shit, get a grip!* she screamed to herself. Ready to go, her mind went completely blank and the program on the screen looked completely foreign to her.

After a few minutes of her staring at the screen like a complete idiot, Sloan leaned down, putting one hand on the back of her chair as the other one pointed.

"Find Adam's name in this row and click." Sloan's voice was so masculine it sent shivers down her spine.

"Stop it," she whispered to herself.

"What?" Sloan glanced at her, their faces close.

"Ah..." was all she could think to say, then snapped her head back to the computer and clicked Adam's name. Thank God, it was coming back to her. For a minute, she thought her brain had gone to shit. Going through the motions with Sloan watching and smelling so damn good, she reached the last step. Becky glanced up at him. "Hit Submit?"

He looked down at her. "Looks good." He nodded, his eyes then focusing on the screen.

"You sure?" Becky hesitated. "I'd really hate to mess up his pay, even though he's less likely to kill me than the other ones."

Sloan chuckled. "It's fine, go ahead."

Becky held her breath and hit Submit. She did a few more with Sloan standing over her. While she was glad he was watching, she also wished he would just go. His closeness was driving her insane and making her a nervous wreck. And she was seriously considering jumping on him. Oh yes she was, and that was not good. Suddenly the screen flashed.

"Uh-oh, what did I do?" Becky frowned, searching the screen frantically.

"Here." Sloan grabbed her hand with the mouse and moved it, then used his finger to pressure hers to click. With no warning whatsoever, the scene from *Ghost* popped into her thoughts, the Patrick Swayze and Demi Moore pottery wheel scene. Oh my God, she was going to lose her shit. No, she'd already lost it.

Thank God the door opened. Sloan released her hand and turned as she sat with her eyes squeezed tightly shut, cursing at herself to stop picturing him sitting behind her playing with her mouse. With that thought a snicker escaped her mouth. It wasn't funny, but dammit, it was. She was so screwed, and that truly wasn't funny.

******

Sloan turned to see Sid walk in with Jared and Jax following. Hearing Becky snicker, he looked back down at her, but she seemed to be focused on the computer.

"You think you got it?" he asked, his gaze going to her hand, which had felt so soft and small under his.

"I'm good," she replied without looking up at him.

"What are you two up to?" Sid moseyed back, looking at the computer. "Hey, don't forget about that raise. Just add a few thousand to mine monthly, Becky babe."

"The only raise you're going to get is my foot up your ass." Sloan nudged him away from Becky.

"Just make sure you don't mess mine up," Jared warned, peeking over her shoulder.

"Then don't make me mad," Becky teased, but didn't look away from the screen. "I have passwords now and know how to use them."

Sloan grinned at her comeback, then looked at the Warriors, who were staring at him. He replaced the grin with a scowl in record time. "What the fuck do you want?"

"So, how's the new secretary working out?" Sid wiggled his eyebrows while Jax and Jared chuckled.

Ignoring Sid, Sloan walked to his desk and sat down, looking at Jax. "What's the progress on the trainees?"

Jax frowned. "We have one missing in action."

"What?" Sloan had picked up his phone to check messages, but turned to look back at Jax.

"Katrina took off during training last night." Jax frowned, anger radiating from him. "It seems the other trainees think she's whoring herself to the Warriors for special treatment."

"Oh, my God. Those assholes," Becky blurted, looking up from the computer. Her eyes widened. "Sorry." She cringed, then went back to work.

"Actually, my thought exactly," Jax grumbled. "Blaze has been looking for her all night with no luck."

"Did you call in Adam?" Sloan knew by the looks on their faces they hadn't.

"And that's why he's the boss man." Sid thumbed toward Sloan.

"Son of a bitch." Jax pulled out his phone, but when Blaze walked through the door, he put it away. "Any luck?"

"No, nothing." Blaze growled, his hands fisting at his sides.

"Call Adam and see if he can get a read on her," Jax told Blaze.

"He's on his way in now." Sloan put down his phone.

"Is there anything you can't do?" Sid looked at Sloan as if in awe. "Did you know, Becky babe, your boss is awesomesauce."

"What are you, an eight-year-old girl?" Becky snorted, shaking her head, still looking at her screen. "And my last name isn't babe, it's Spencer. Call me Becky babe one more time and I'm filing sexual harassment charges."

Sid frowned and looked at Sloan. "Can she do that?"

Sloan nodded, his eyebrow cocked. "Yes, she can." He looked back at Becky, who was grinning behind her computer screen. He could tell because her eyes were crinkled at the corners. Yeah, she could handle these assholes pretty well. He was actually impressed.

"Well played, Becky Spencer." Jared smiled with an approving nod. "Well played.

"Thank you." Becky beamed, then laughed when Sid turned his frown toward her.

"What's up?" Adam walked in, looking at everyone.

"Katrina took off last night," Sloan answered before anyone else could. "Can you get a read on where she might be?"

"I'm sure I can." Adam frowned. "Why? What happened?"

"The other trainees think she's whoring herself out to the Warriors for special treatment," Jax answered, his eyes going to Blaze, who growled.

"Who the fuck's saying that?" Adam's voice rose. "Katrina is the sweetest person. She would never do something like that. I'll fucking kick someone's ass. Who the fuck said it?"

"Slow down, killer." Jax stood. "We're taking care of it, but we need to know where she is."

Adam walked away as everyone became quiet, watching him.

"She's at a Dollar General," Adam replied. "Not sure which one, but there is one about five minutes from here on Taft."

"Thanks, man." Blaze was already heading for the door.

"Are you going to force her back?" Becky still sat working, but was frowning at Blaze. "Because honestly, if it was me in her situation, I wouldn't want to come back under these circumstances."

"She's coming back." Blaze once again headed toward the door, but stopped and turned. "How would you handle it?"

Sloan sat back, arms crossed, and when Becky glanced his way, he gave her a nod to continue. Maybe Jill had been onto something with this secretary shit.

Chapter 11

Well, crap, she hadn't expected to be asked what she would do. So why in the hell did she open her big mouth? It was only her second day, for shit's sake. Her eyes shot to Sloan's, but all he did was give her a nod like, "go for it." Everyone was staring at her and all she could do was stare back.

"Well, ah...." She cleared her throat. "I mean, I don't know exactly what to do, but I know being a woman and if I had peers thinking I was... you know... whoring around, I would be very uncomfortable going back into that situation."

"Well, that's kind of a no-brainer, Becky," Sid replied with a snort.

"Ah, did I hurt your feelings with the eight-year-old little girl comment, Sid?" Becky's attitude turned from helpful to sarcastic in a flash. Taking a deep breath, she calmed herself. "Sorry, I was voted most outspoken smartass in high school."

Jared snorted and Sid actually laughed. "Well, welcome to the family." Jared grinned.

"She's right." Jared glanced at Blaze. "Forcing Katrina to come back after something like that isn't going to do her any good. We need a plan of action."

Becky stood, feeling a little more confident with Jared on her side. "So what makes them think she's getting special attention?"

"She lives here at the compound for one," Adam replied. "I know me, Jill, and Steve got some shit about that from other trainees, but we just shut them up. Katrina hasn't reached that point to be able to do that yet, and there were three of us."

"Then maybe you guys need to show up some to keep the other trainees busy so they can't think of anything other than picking their asses off the floor." Becky was getting into this; maybe she had missed her calling. She should have been an advisor to a bunch of hot warriors. "That way whoever is doing the training doesn't look like they are standing up for her all the time. Plus, having another girl in there may help. I've heard Jill is a badass."

"That's actually not a bad idea." Jax cocked his brow. "Can we clear their schedules for a few weeks? Katrina does need some extra help."

"Consider it done," Sloan replied, his focus on Becky.

Becky tried to hide how pleased she was that he'd not only considered her idea, but "considered it done." Ugh, there she went again, being happy she'd pleased a man. It had to stop, but she knew it wouldn't. She was a pleaser, always had been.

"I don't think there is anything we can do about her living arrangements though," Adam added. "Steve said she was homeless before coming here."

Becky thought about it for a second. "She could stay with me."

"That's not your responsibility." Sloan shook his head.

"No, but it's a solution," Becky added, then shrugged. "I mean, you saw my place. I don't have a lot of room, but it could work okay."

"Whoa, what?" Sid sat up straight, showing more interest. "The boss man has been to your place?"

Becky looked at Sid, confused, then saw Sloan's subtle cringe. "Oh, wait." Becky rolled her eyes. "I forgot. We're not all adults here."

"Ouch." Jared snapped his head back, but grinned.

"We'll figure it out later." Blaze turned to Adam. "Is she still there or has she moved to another state during all the bullshit?"

"So much hate." Sid stood and stretched. "Just curious about why the boss man was at the secretary's place already. Seems a little soon to be —"

Sloan was around his desk and had Sid against the wall so fast Becky almost fell over moving out of the way. "I don't care how big of a badass you think you are, if you disrespect her again, you will regret ever meeting me. Her name is Becky, not secretary or babe, and there is nothing going on between us."

"Jesus, Sid." Jared was ready to pull them apart. "Learn to shut your fucking mouth before you get killed."

Sid ignored Jared, his eyes black as night. "Funny how the tables turn." Sid grinned, but then nodded. "Okay. Okay, can you let me go so I can apologize?"

"Watch your step, Sinclair," Sloan warned before letting him go.

"I hear you loud and clear, boss man." Sid straightened his shirt after Sloan let him go.

"Get used to this shit," Jax whispered to her as she stood staring at Sloan and Sid wide-eyed. "I'd say twice, maybe three times a week you'll see somebody slamming somebody in this office. Just stay in your corner and you'll be safe."

"Holy shit," Becky croaked before she looked up at Jax. "Guess it won't be boring."

Jax laughed in agreement. "Never."

She watched Sid head her way. "Please accept my apology, my lady." Sid grinned down at her. "I meant nothing by it."

Becky narrowed her eyes at him before she smiled. She couldn't help it. "Yes, you did." She shook her head. "You're a handful, aren't you?"

"You have no idea." He winked at her before putting on a straight face and walking out of the office.

She watched everyone else leave behind Sid, except for Blaze, who must have left during the excitement. Sloan was still standing, but he was glaring at her.

"I guess I should have kept my mouth shut." Becky bit her lip. He didn't look very happy. "I seem to have a problem with my mouth." Okay, that sounded... weird.

Sloan's eyes darkened as they traveled to her mouth, but then he looked away and headed for his desk. "You're fine," he responded, grabbing his phone and a set of keys. "After you finish the payroll, you can leave."

"Okay." Becky frowned when he walked out, slamming the door behind him. "Well, shit. You really need to learn how to keep your mouth shut, Spencer. Day two on the job and you're already showing your ass," she told herself as she went to finish the payroll. She glanced at her phone to see the time. It looked like she was going to take her time, since it wasn't even noon yet.

With a sigh she sat down, her eyes going to Sloan's desk. Suddenly the room felt very empty, and that was not good at all. She was missing her boss.

******

Sloan slammed out of his office. "Jax!" Sloan growled, then took a breath to calm down.

"Yeah." Jax stopped, turning toward him.

"I want all the trainees at the warehouse in an hour, as well as any Warrior that's available."

"Yes, sir." Jax nodded, pulling out his phone as he disappeared down the hall.

Sloan headed out to his bike, climbed on, and took off toward the warehouse. He needed to work out. He had too much energy and he was pissed at himself. After a short a three-minute ride, he was inside at his locker changing into sweats. Looking around, he couldn't find a shirt.

"Fuck it." He walked out of the locker room, not bothering to find gloves or wraps as he headed for one of the many heavy bags hanging throughout the warehouse. Doing some warm-up on the bag, he cursed some more.

What in the fuck was wrong with him? He'd almost killed Sid for no apparent reason. The fucker had pissed him off with worse shit than what he'd just done in his office, yet Sloan had been ready to pull a Damon and snap his fucking head off.

The more he thought, the harder he hit the bag with everything he had. Elbows, fists, knees, kicks, and once that bag ripped, he went to the next. He knew exactly what was going on, yet he fought it. He didn't have time for this shit. The first time he had seen Becky Spencer, the day of Jill's big interview fiasco, he'd been drawn to her and hadn't been able to stop thinking of her. Even as busy as he was, his thoughts would regularly drift to her.

Another bag busted and he moved on to the next. He pounded the bags nonstop. When Caroline had suggested her for the job, he had fought it, even though the thought of having Becky near soothed him. What the fuck! He spun and kicked the bag so hard it hit the wall and stuck. And on to the next he went.

She was a beautiful woman, but that wasn't it. He was drawn to her like no other woman, and he'd had plenty of women. None of them had ever made him think twice about them, sad as that was. He hadn't even touched her sexually, yet he couldn't get enough.

"Motherfucker," Sloan roared, pounding the bag in frustration. As much shit as he had given his mated Warriors, it was going to bite him in the ass if he wasn't careful. He had no room in his life for a mate, a human mate at that. He was not mate material. He knew that. Though deep down, he wanted it even knowing he couldn't have it.

With another roar, he struck out with a spinning back fist. The bag broke from the chain and landed a few feet away. Glancing at the destruction, Sloan cracked his neck back and forth before turning to find all the trainees staring at him in awe and the Warriors grinning like idiots.

"What the fuck you doing just standing there?" Sloan took a step toward them. "Get out here and take a knee."

The trainees tripped over themselves and each other trying to get out on the floor quickly enough, each kneeling. Wide eyed, they stared up at one huge, pissed off Sloan Murphy.

"I'm going to say this one time and if I have to repeat myself, someone is going to die." Sloan actually took time to look each trainee in the eye. "We are a unit. I may want to beat the shit out of one of my Warriors on a daily basis, but I've got their back and they've got mine. We have a problem with each other, we talk it out or fight it out and then it's done. What we do not do is go around like little bitches talking about each other or making assumptions that we don't fucking know."

"Yes, sir." The trainees spoke in unison.

"None of you are warrior material in my eyes, so you're damn lucky I don't make many appearances here, but if shit don't change and change immediately, you are going to see me here on a daily basis and that, you assholes, will not be pleasant for you."

"Yes, sir." Their response was louder, echoing around the building.

"Who is the one who started the rumor about Katrina?" No one answered, but a few glanced toward one trainee. "This rumor is going to stop. Is that understood?"

"Yes, sir."

"You have questioned not only my Warriors, but my integrity that we would take advantage of a woman who would whore herself to get special treatment." Sloan growled, his eyes narrowed. "I'm so fucking close to kicking all your asses out of here and getting real men who know when to keep their fucking mouths closed and how to respect a woman and each other."

"Yes, sir." This time there was doubt in their tone.

"Now, I'm going to ask one more fucking time who started this shit about Katrina." Sloan once again looked at all the trainees, but saved the one he knew was guilty for last. "Are you going to be a man and own up to this, because if not, get the fuck out of my warehouse."

"I suggested it but everyone agreed." Ben's voice shook as he stood, his eyes not meeting Sloan's. "I didn't mean anything by it."

"No one gets special treatment," Sloan announced loudly. "Just ask Jill." He nodded behind them.

They turned to look at Jill who stood, her face pinched in anger.

"As a matter of fact, she, along with the new Warriors who just finished this program, will be here to teach you pussies what's really important." Sloan's tone turned cold. "So if you don't think you can handle training and you're only good at talking about another teammate, then I suggest you not come back tonight."

"Yes, sir."

Sloan's eyes slammed into Ben. "And as for you." Sloan took three steps to stand directly in front of him. "Katrina will be the one deciding your fate in this program."

Ben nodded. "Yes, sir."

Sloan looked at the Warriors present. "I want them too fucking tired to even talk and any problems, I want to know ASAP."

The Warriors nodded, each looking pissed, but ready to teach a hard lesson.

Once again after looking at each trainee in the eye, Sloan growled, "Get the fuck out of here."

They didn't hesitate. In a second flat, the only ones remaining were the Warriors. Sloan didn't say a word to any of them. He turned and headed for the locker room. He'd said his piece and he really didn't need to hear any shit about the heavy bags he had killed.

Chapter 12

Katrina walked down the wet, slippery hill through the wooded area behind the store. The building of the Dollar General came into view. The reason she had picked this place when she first had nowhere to go was because of the wooded area. It was easy to stay hidden from view during the store's busy hours. She had been spotted earlier by one of the workers so she had taken off.

Walking toward the tarp she had found and used as a makeshift shelter, she tossed her bag containing all her belongings under it and then sat down. Her stomach tightened painfully. She needed to feed, and soon. It was bad enough that she was hungry for blood, but she still needed other nourishment. A pizza sounded awesome and she moaned, lying back in the wet leaves. She stared up at the tarp, through the hole and through the trees that were losing their leaves to the sky. It was a typical fall sky. The clouds were billowy, some white, some dark, and behind the clouds the sky was a beautiful dark blue.

Feeling something tickle her fingers, she moved her head to see a rabbit sniffing her. She loved animals, always had since she was a little girl. She had been drawn to them and they to her, but after she was changed, she'd developed an understanding that had terrified her and still did a little. She hadn't understood it until she was with the Warriors and she'd heard them talk about powers. She guessed her power was with animals. Then again, she didn't really know if that was true. She had been afraid to say anything. What if it wasn't a power and she was just strange? She had enough going against her without adding more to it.

"How has your day been so far, Bugs?" She grinned at the name she'd given the rabbit.

Bugs looked up from her fingers, tilting its furry head.

"Ma'am," a male voice called out.

The rabbit scurried away as Katrina sat straight up. Two police officers stood a few feet away. Her eyes scanned to find the quickest escape, but one of the officers held up his hand.

"Please don't run." He frowned. "We were called by the manager. He said he can't have you living behind the store." His eyes took in the surroundings. "Are you living back here?" he asked, his eyes and voice kind.

Fear thrummed through Katrina; she didn't want to go to jail, but knew she was breaking the law. "No," she lied, not knowing what else to do.

"Come on, ma'am." The other police officer took a step forward, causing Katrina to jump to her feet.

"I'll leave." Katrina slowly reached down to grab her bag. "I'll leave," she repeated a little more frantically. Seeing movement out of the corner of her eye, she saw the huge deer camouflaged, watching, waiting. Slowly she shook her head, then looked back toward the officers.

"We can take you somewhere to get something to eat." He reached out his hand, waving her toward him. "We can also call the VC Warriors and see if they can help you."

"No!" At the mention of the Warriors, Katrina was ready to bolt.

"No need," a familiar voice came from behind the officers. "We're already here."

******

Blaze had left the compound and headed straight toward where Adam said Katrina was. Pulling into the parking lot, he looked around but saw no sign of her. Parking, he climbed off the bike and started to head inside, until he'd heard voices. Following the sound, he'd continued until he saw two uniformed police officers and Katrina.

She stood next to a tarp she must have set up to try to stay out of the rain the previous night. Fuck, why hadn't he thought of Adam sooner? Glancing at her surroundings, he was pissed that she'd felt this was better than being at the compound. Nothing about this was safe for a woman, even a full-blooded vampire. She would be no match against a male vampire and there were plenty running around this part of town. It was the reason it was heavily patrolled by Warriors.

He watched as her eyes moved from the officers to something in the trees. His eyes followed. A large buck stood hidden, but its eyes were on her. He looked back to see her shake her head discreetly before looking back at the officers. The large buck took a step back as if following her orders. *Interesting.*

Turning his attention back to Katrina, he heard the officers say they were going to call in the Warriors to help her.

"No need." He stepped forward, his eyes on Katrina. "We're already here."

When Katrina's eyes popped wide staring at him, he cocked his eyebrow at her. As the officers came his way, he reached out and shook their hands, glancing at their name tags.

"I will be sure to let Sloan know how helpful you were to one of our own." Blaze nodded.

"There's no way we could keep a handle on all this without you guys," one of them replied. "If there isn't anything else we can do, I'll let the manger know it's been taken care of."

Blaze nodded, watching them go before turning toward Katrina. "So where should we start?" Blaze asked. When Katrina remained silent, he continued, "Why you ran or your Dr. Doolittle moment with the large buck who is glaring at me?"

As her eyes darted for escape, he knew she was ready to run, yet he stood there.

"I will catch you," he warned, but stayed relaxed and at ease.

"Why are you here?" she asked, her shoulders slumping in defeat.

And wasn't that the question of the day. Blaze had asked himself that same exact question the previous night as he'd hunted for her nonstop. Why? He didn't have the answer, or at least the answer he wanted to hear.

"You're going to make us late for training," Blaze responded, not answering her question. "Now let's go."

"I'm not going back." Katrina shook her head, her mouth set in a stubborn line.

"Should I call the officers back?" Blaze threw out, cocking his eyebrow. He knew he wouldn't do that, but she didn't.

"Why?" Katrina frowned, throwing her arms out. "Why do you even care? I can take care of myself and have been doing it for a long time."

"Because you're my responsibility," Blaze replied without hesitation.

"No, I'm not." Katrina's voice rose, which was something he had never heard. "So you can just walk away with a clear conscience because I am no one's responsibility."

"You belong in the program, Katrina." Blaze's eyes narrowed. He didn't want to force her back, but he'd be damn if he left her to live behind a fucking Dollar General store.

She actually laughed. "I'm the worst trainee you have, Blaze. And I will not walk back in knowing my peers think I'm whoring myself to rise in the ranks." She looked around at her surroundings, her makeshift camp. She released a bitter laugh. "It may not look like I have much pride, but I do."

"And that is exactly why you belong in this program," Blaze shot back. "To prove that you belong."

"Really? Do I really belong?" Katrina sighed. "And I'm done proving myself to everyone. That is all I've done in my life, prove something to someone who cares nothing for me. It doesn't matter what I do. I'm still invisible except when I do something right, and then I'm accused of being a whore."

Blaze watched her cringe, knowing she'd said more than she'd wanted. He didn't like being in the position of not knowing what the fuck to do. She was right. Why would she put herself in that position again? It was bullshit, yet there he was asking her to do it.

"What if you didn't live at the compound?" Blaze tilted his head. "What if everything that made it look like you were getting special treatment was gone and you walked in as an equal."

"It wouldn't matter," Katrina said, but there was hope in her eyes. He saw it and he was going to run with it.

"I once heard you say this was something you wanted to do, something you wanted to accomplish. Do you think Jill would have given up? Do you think Jill had it easy?" Blaze was grasping for anything to get through to her.

"I'm not Jill." Katrina frowned. "And yes, it was something I wanted. Things change. Things always change."

"Exactly," Blaze replied, taking a step toward her. "Things do change and sometimes it takes us to change them to what we want. You can do this, Katrina. If I didn't believe that, I wouldn't be here."

He watched the emotions play across her face. He knew she wanted this, so he would fight for her only because that was part of his job as a trainer. He would be doing the same thing for any of the trainees. He kept telling himself that same lie over and over again. When she remained silent, he frowned, watching her arm wrap around her stomach.

"Have you eaten?" His eyes remained on her stomach when she snapped her arm away. His eyes rose to meet hers, but she looked away. "I asked you a question, Katrina."

"A little," she replied, still not looking at him.

"Come on." He stretched his arm out, waving her to him. "Let's go eat. I'm also hungry. We can talk some more because honestly, that damn buck staring me down is making me a little nervous."

Katrina turned to look and then shook her head. "He won't hurt you."

"And you know that how?" Blaze had a feeling he knew how, but wanted to hear it from her.

She looked back at him. "Because I told him not to."

Chapter 13

Becky had changed into a pair of shorts and a T-shirt when she'd arrived home, then started cleaning. She had done everything she could think of at work to stay longer, but boredom finally won and she'd left. She had wanted to wait until Sloan returned so she could apologize for opening her big mouth... again. Her mouth was cursed, spouting shit with no filter.

Grabbing a rubber band out of her junk drawer, she put her hair in a ponytail. It was hot for mid-September. Opening her front door, she locked the screen, then opened up her windows.

She had talked to Frankie on her way home. He was loving college and had made new friends. His classes were going great, as was his new job. His father had finally sent him the money for the books he needed, but had bribed Frankie into going to see him during his first three-day weekend off. It bothered her that her ex did stuff like that, but she knew Frankie would make his way to her house anyway.

Heading to the kitchen, she grabbed the furniture polish under the kitchen sink, but stood up quickly when she heard a motorcycle. Her stomach dipped and her heart sped up. When it sounded as if it stopped in front of her house, her breathing quickened. Holy shit, just the sound of a motorcycle was going to make her orgasm. Bending so she could look out the front door, she sighed, seeing Sloan slipping off his bike. She had been wrong. It wasn't the motorcycle; it was the man riding the motorcycle.

She held the furniture polish close to her chest, watching him walk toward her door. The way he carried himself with no-nonsense purpose made her wish she was lying in bed naked with him walking toward her like that. Yes, she went there. How could she not? The man oozed sex like no other.

"No men, my ass." She snorted at herself and rolled her eyes. The knock that she knew was coming startled her anyway, making her spray the furniture polish toward her face. "Shit!"

Setting the polish on the table, she headed for the door, using the bottom of her T-shirt to wipe the polish off her chin. Reaching the door, she came face-to-face with Sloan, who was staring at her bare stomach. Dropping the shirt, she reached out to unlock and open the door.

"Hey." She stepped aside, letting him in. "Everything okay?"

He nodded and walked in. Then turning toward her, he looked at the lock on the screen door. "Do you really think locking that thing will keep anyone out?"

"Never really thought about it before." She frowned at the lock. "Thanks for freaking me out though."

"You need better locks." Sloan frowned, ignoring her sarcasm. "Did you really mean you'd let Katrina stay here for a little bit?"

"Yes, I did," Becky replied, glancing around her small house. "I mean I don't have a lot of room, obviously. But it could work and it's a little lonely with Frankie gone now."

"I'll pay your rent—"

"No, you won't." Becky frowned. "I offered to let her stay. Done deal."

"Along with your electric and water," Sloan finished, ignoring her refusal.

"No, don't think so," Becky shot back. "I have a job now, unless I'm fired."

Sloan seemed ready to say something, but stopped, his eyes narrowing. "Why would you be fired?"

"I think I pissed my boss off." Becky cringed, then shrugged. "He sent me home early. I guess I should have warned my boss during the interview that I'm outspoken. I also usually say anything that comes to my mind. I have no filter, never have. Not a very good trait in a woman to most—"

"It's a trait I respect." Sloan stopped her. "You're not fired, but your boss has a short fuse at times and it's best to just step out of the way."

"You got that right." She snorted, then her eyes popped open wide. She pointed to herself. "See, no filter."

Sloan actually grinned. "Blaze and Katrina will be here any minute."

"He found her?" Becky sighed in relief.

Nodding, Sloan leaned against the wall, crossing his arms. "Are you sure about this?"

"Of course, I'm sure." Becky also crossed her arms, but across her breasts. Her nipples were going a little crazy, reacting to the way Sloan's eyes kept going to her bare legs. Actually, her nipples weren't the only things going a little crazy. "I wouldn't have offered if I wasn't sure."

He only nodded, a small hint of a smile tipping his lips. Holy crap on a cracker, she needed to get a grip. His silence was driving her nuts and she was never without anything to say… ever. What in the hell was he doing to her?

"You know, anytime I get on your nerves by stating my opinions, you can tell me to, you know…," Becky said, not able to stay silent. She guessed he was waiting for Blaze and Katrina, but the quiet gave her mind time to think of very inappropriate things she'd like to do to her boss. And that was a huge no-no with him standing right smack in front of her. Those thoughts were best saved for when she was alone, very alone.

"Oh, I will." Sloan cocked an eyebrow at her.

"Well, okay. Good," Becky replied, then screamed at herself to just shut the hell up. Hearing another motorcycle, she prayed it was Blaze. It was then she realized her body didn't react to the sound like it had earlier. Her eyes went from the window back to Sloan, who was still staring at her.

They stood quietly as the motorcycle passed on by. Crap, it wasn't them. Cars passed up and down the road. Everyday life happened outside her small house on her busy road while they just stood inside without saying anything. Becky couldn't remember a more awkward time in her life. Obviously Sloan wasn't down for small talk.

He made her feel tiny inside her house. He filled it with authority and a maleness no woman could deny. Glancing down at her bare feet, then to his large boots, she sighed. He was a big man and she wondered stupidly with him standing there if he was big everywhere.

A motorcycle pulled up to her house and stopped. "They're here," Becky said quickly and a little loudly as her head snapped up. "Thank God," she whispered as she headed toward the door.

******

Sloan grinned, hearing her whispered words. He had watched her checking him out, but doing her best to hide the fact. He had stayed silent for a reason and he knew it drove her nuts, but fair was fair because those cut-off shorts were driving him completely in-fucking-sane.

He turned and watched her open the door for Blaze and Katrina. She was openly excited to meet the small girl who had stolen the Warriors' hearts and their mates'. He knew Katrina's life had been hard, but that was her story to tell. He was going to make damn sure she passed the Warrior training. Jill had changed his mind about women Warriors. He knew they could be just as valuable as the men. Obviously, he would never let Jill know that.

"I think we kind of met during the interviews for Sloan's secretary, but honestly, I'm not sure. That was a little crazy." Becky smiled, letting them in. "So, I'm Becky Spencer and it's really nice meeting you, Katrina."

"Thank you, it's nice meeting you," Katrina replied, her eyes going directly to Sloan before snapping to the ground.

Before Sloan could say anything, Becky elbowed him in the side. He glared down at her and she nodded toward Katrina. "Say something," she whispered.

He bent toward her. "Remember when you told me to let you know if you were getting on my nerves?" Sloan's eyes narrowed.

"So soon." Becky bit her lip. Nodding, she turned her attention back to Katrina and Blaze. "Anyone need something to drink?"

Katrina shook her head.

"We just had something," Blaze replied. "Thanks."

"No problem." Becky stepped into the kitchen and busied herself.

Sloan again grinned, but wiped it off his face when he noticed Blaze staring at him. "So, Katrina." Sloan waited until Katrina lifted her face to meet his gaze. "What do you want?"

Katrina let her eyes roam his as if searching for the answer. "I don't know what you mean, sir."

"Well, let me make it easy on you," Sloan replied, his voice stern. "Do you want to continue living on the streets or do you want to become a respected VC Warrior? Because this is the last chance you have before I make the decision for you. Living on the streets is harsh, but if that's what you want to do then get the fuck out of here and stop wasting our time."

Becky gasped and Sloan knew she was ready to open her mouth, but his hand flew up, stopping her. Blaze was also glaring at him, but he ignored it. His focus never left Katrina and he was glad because he saw a spark of something in her eyes, and it wasn't a sign of giving up.

"Have you ever lived on the streets?" Katrina asked after a few minutes of tense silence, her voice void of any emotions.

"Yes," Sloan replied.

"Then you know no one would choose to live on the streets." Katrina continued to stare at him. "Neither would someone put themselves in a situation where they were treated as if they were a whore."

"Truth," Becky added, then snapped her mouth closed when Sloan turned to look at her over his shoulder. "Sorry." She acted as if she zipped her lips closed.

"That will not be happening again." Sloan turned his attention back to Katrina. "I personally made sure of that."

Katrina actually looked at Becky, then closed her eyes. "Now they will hate me even more."

"Then work your ass off to make sure they have no reason to hate you except when you kick *their* ass." Becky gave her a nod. "Come on, Katrina. I mean, I don't know you, but it sounds like these guys are just a bunch of jealous drama queens, who for some reason are intimidated by you."

Sloan watched Becky's words sink in, so he stepped back and let Becky continue.

Katrina shook her head. "They are not intimidated by me."

"Obviously they are if you're the only thing they have to talk about." Becky raised an eyebrow at her. "If it were me, I'd be in there 24-7 to prove those assholes wrong. I bet Jill will help you. It seems she'd like to stick it to a bunch of idiots."

"You think she would?" Katrina looked up at Sloan, hopeful.

"It's already taken care of," Sloan replied, his respect for his new secretary soaring. She'd done in a second flat what he and Blaze couldn't do, give this girl with no confidence whatsoever, hope. "She will be there tomorrow."

Everyone watched a battle rage across Katrina's face until she finally nodded. "Okay."

"Good." Sloan gave one short nod. "You will be staying here with Becky instead of the compound until you officially become a Warrior. I expect you back at tomorrow's session. You can ride in with Becky on her way to work."

"Thank you," she said, first to Sloan and then Becky.

"Ben started the rumor and has everyone going on it," Sloan added, his eyes staring her down. "It is up to you, right now, if he stays in the program."

"I don't want anyone kicked out because of me," Katrina finally replied, her voice and eyes not wavering.

"Good girl." Becky gave her a thumbs-up.

"There's something else you should know." Blaze stepped in. "It looks like Katrina has a power that I've never heard of."

"Which is?" Sloan's interest piqued. Any powers, even odd, helped their fight against the war going on that grew worse every day.

"Seems we have our own Dr. Dolittle," Blaze replied, a small grin tipping his lips.

"Who the fuck is Dr. Dolittle?" Sloan frowned, not having a clue what Blaze was talking about.

"Holy crap." Becky stepped next to Sloan with a huge grin on her face. "You can talk to animals?"

"Who the fuck is Dr. Dolittle?" Sloan repeated, still not getting it.

"You know, Eddie Murphy, the movie." Becky glared up at him. "Seriously, you need a movie night."

Sloan ignored her, but chuckled to himself. Lord, he was truly fucked with her. No one in the room knew what he was thinking because he made damn sure he looked serious enough to kill anything that moved. "So you are telling me you can talk to animals?"

Katrina nodded.

Sloan had heard of some strange powers, but this was a new one even for him. "Okay, you know what, let's save this until tomorrow when all the Warriors are present."

"Sounds good," Blaze replied. "She needs to feed anyway."

"Oh, I just went to the store," Becky spoke up. "I can make something real quick."

"Not for food," Sloan replied, liking the way Becky was ready to jump in and help one of his Warriors and future Warrior, with not just food, but opening her home. Not many would do that, but she was different and in the short time he had known her, his respect for her was growing, quickly.

"Huh?" Becky looked at him for a second until understanding brightened her face. "Oh! Well, yeah, ah, I don't have any of that."

Sloan actually laughed, a real belly laugh. How fucking long had it been since he'd done that. Long enough that he couldn't remember.

"Where's your bathroom?" Blaze also chuckled as he took Katrina's arm.

"Right down that hall." Becky pointed and when they disappeared, she rolled her eyes. "Thought that was funny, did you?"

"Very," Sloan agreed, then watched her start cleaning.

"Well, I'm learning all about this vampire stuff." Becky sprayed polish on her coffee table and started wiping it off. "Give me a week and I'll have it all down."

"I have no doubt," Sloan replied, his eyes on her ass as it swayed with each swipe of the cloth. He also had no doubts that he would be having that sooner than later, no matter how long he fought it. He was a smart man and knew where this was headed; he just didn't know where it would lead and that was stopping him from grabbing her right then.

"How long does it take?" Becky had turned around and was looking at him.

"What?" Sloan's eyes rose to meet hers.

"You know." She waved her cloth toward the bathroom.

"Feeding?" Sloan's eyebrow rose. "Only a few minutes unless…." *Shit.* He stopped himself.

"What?" Becky pried. "Unless what?"

"Nothing." Sloan cursed, knowing she wasn't going to drop it. "Feeding between two people who have an attraction to each other can be…."

"Sexual?" Becky added, her eyes widened. "Interesting. So do they have an attraction?"

"How the hell should I know?" Sloan griped. "I don't keep track of my Warriors' love life shit."

"I think they do. I mean, Blaze is one hell of a man and she is so cute. They'd make an adorable couple." Becky had ignored his pissy reply. "My bathroom's pretty small though."

Before Sloan could reply, which he was ready to do because he did not like her saying Blaze was one hell of a man like she wouldn't mind having him in her bed and that pissed him off, Blaze and Katrina appeared.

"Well, that was fast." Becky actually looked disappointed.

Sloan was ready to get the hell out of there. She was confusing the fuck out of him and he was ready to do or say something stupid.

"You ready?" he asked Blaze, who nodded. Then Sloan looked at Becky. "Is there anything else you might need?"

"Nope, I think we're good. We'll just get to know each other. Maybe call on some animals, because how cool is that." Becky gave him a teasing grin.

"Stay out of trouble," Sloan warned, walking out the door behind Blaze.

"How much trouble can two redheads get into anyway?" She looked over and winked at Katrina. "We'll be fine. See you tomorrow."

"So about this power you have?" Becky's voice carried out to Sloan and Blaze.

Both men looked at each other, shaking their heads. "This may have been a bad idea." Sloan frowned, getting on his bike.

"Guess we'll find out soon enough." Blaze looked back at the house before mounting his bike, backing out, and taking off.

Sloan glanced once more to see Becky watching him from the door. Surprise filtered through him at how quickly things were escalating between him and the redhead. For once it wasn't just about sex. Revving his bike, he took off, hurrying toward the road where he could let loose, wondering if he could outrun his feelings.

Chapter 14

It didn't take long for Becky and Katrina to hit it off. Katrina was softly spoken, very intelligent, and funny. It was getting late so Becky started closing the windows and locking up. The bar across the street was packed even on a week night, but that was nothing new for Becky, though she noticed Katrina kept looking out the window that way.

"You get used to the noise." Becky smiled at Katrina. "Sometimes when they have a good band it's kind of nice. I go over there sometimes to do karaoke, which is fun."

"I've never done karaoke before." Katrina looked away from the bar.

"Seriously?" Becky walked over an d sat in the chair across from Katrina, who sat on the couch. "Are you twenty-one yet?"

"No, not for a couple more months." Katrina seemed to finally relax, pulling her bare feet under her.

"We are going to have to go over one night during karaoke." Becky's voice rose in excitement. Her friend list had diminished when she and Frank divorced. It was especially nice to talk to someone of her gender. "You can still get in, but you can't drink."

"That's fine. I don't drin k anyway." Katrina glanced away, looking uncomfortable.

Becky knew something in the girl's past haunted her. She didn't want to pry, yet she wanted her to know that she had a friend. Everyone needed someone.

"Katrina, know that if you ever need to talk, I'm here." Becky gave her a reassuring smile. "I know what's it like when you don't have anyone to talk to."

Katrina swallowed hard as she nodded. "Thank you."

"You're welcome," Becky replied, standing up. "Now, what can we do? I'm not tired enough to go to bed. What about you?"

"I don't sleep." Katrina shrugged, then laughed at Becky's expression. "Don't worry, I don't expect you to stay up with me."

"You know I'm still getting used to the vampire stuff, so bear with me," Becky admitted with a laugh, then glanced at Katrina. "Can I ask you something?"

"Sure."

"Doesn't it freak you out just a little to survive on blood?" Becky asked, then cursed herself for asking after seeing the look on Katrina's face. "Hey, I'm a dumbass. Don't answer that."

"No, it's fine." Katrina actually laughed. "It's not bad if it's from the right person."

"Oh." Becky's eyes popped open. "So say like… Blaze being that right person." Becky wiggled her eyebrows up and down.

Katrina shrugged, embarrassment flashing across her face. "Maybe."

"Damn, girl. You've got taste." Becky nodded in full agreement. "That man is one fine piece of maleness."

"So is Sloan," Katrina shot back with a knowing grin.

"That obvious, am I?" Becky didn't even try to deny her attraction to Sloan Murphy. Hell, what woman wouldn't be attracted to that man? "And you're absolutely right. We both have superb taste in men. After my divorce I told myself no men, but that went right out the damn window."

"Blaze is just being nice," Katrina added quickly. "He would do it for any of the other trainees."

"I seriously doubt that." Becky snorted, but left it at that. "So, how about getting into some trouble?"

"I think I'm already in trouble," Katrina replied, but grinned. "Like what?"

Becky thought for a moment. "Well, there aren't many animals around here, but I really want to see what you can do."

"I honestly don't know exactly what I can do." Katrina frowned, sitting up straighter. "I've always been drawn to animals and then when I was turned into a half-breed, it intensified. And now it seems like I can understand them and they can understand me."

"You're freaking Snow White." Becky clapped her hands together, then stopped. "No, wait. Snow White had the dwarfs. Cinderella had the mice and birds around her, not to mention the handsome prince which Blaze fills in quite nicely."

Katrina laughed, shaking her head. "I'm no Cinderella."

"I bet none of the other trainees have powers like that." Becky's grin turned mischievous. "I think during our free time we should hone that skill you got, Ms. Dolittle."

"You'd help me?" Katrina asked, a hopeful, excited expression lighting her face.

"Hell yeah, I'll help you." Becky grinned, glancing at the clock. "Sleep is overrated anyway. Plus, my life is so boring I need some excitement. Since my son turned teenager, and mom was no longer cool, I've been bored to death. Now he's a man in college, I need some excitement."

"Let's do it." Katrina stood. "I've been wanting to do more but have been afraid."

Becky stepped into her shoes and grabbed her keys. "I know exactly where to go. It's not far from here."

"Can we take the scooter?" Katrina asked, her eyes widening and a pleading look on her face. "I saw it the first day you came to work. I've always wanted to ride one."

Becky thought about it for a second. Ah, hell. What harm would it do? Sloan would never find out anyway. Plus she wasn't alone. She had a vampire with her who could control animals. What could happen?

******

After leaving Becky's, Sloan and Blaze patrolled the area, going to two empty buildings right up from her house. Searching through one of the abandoned buildings for any rogue vampire activity, Sloan frowned. Old blood had soaked into the carpet. The metallic smell had hit them when entering the building.

"You find anything?" Blaze asked, walking into the room.

"Definitely some activity here." Sloan cursed. "No body, so I'm thinking they either hid it or we have another new vampire running around."

"I didn't find anything, so hopefully it was just a single incident." Blaze glanced down at the stained carpet. "Doesn't look recent."

"Probably isn't. This property hasn't been checked for a while." Sloan frowned, hating the fact they were losing the war. Rogue vampires still ran rampant. Crimson Rush was still an issue. Though the selling of children had diminished some, it was not enough to ease his peace of mind. And there was always someone wanting to take down the Warriors. They didn't have enough Warriors to search every abandoned building, and rechecking them took months as the bad guys moved to new buildings.

"No, but these boarded-up buildings are breeding grounds, literally." Sloan headed out of the room with Blaze following until they were outside.

"When's the new Warrior starting?" Blaze kicked over a mattress to check underneath.

"Next week," Sloan replied, looking over at Blaze. "So when are you going to let me reinstate you to Warrior status?"

"Never," Blaze replied without looking at him, his voice final.

"Not making it easy on me to do the paperwork." Sloan grimaced, wishing Blaze would just forget about the past and move on, but that probably would never happen.

"Well, guess it's a good thing you got a secretary now to handle that for you," Blaze added with a sideways glare, making it clear he was done with the conversation.

Before Sloan could say another word, a familiar sound hit his ears. "You have got to be shitting me."

Blaze followed him toward the street. "What?"

Both men stood watching as a bright pink scooter passed them with two very familiar redheads laughing and talking loudly as they passed. Without saying a word, they hurried around the corner to where their motorcycles were parked, both furious.

Chapter 15

Becky pulled into the small park and noticed the gate was closed. Glancing around, she didn't see any cameras. There were no cars were out and about this late, so she went around the gate, which was easy to do on a scooter, totally ignoring the CLOSED AT DUSK sign. She turned out her single headlight and headed toward Licking River. Stopping, she parked and hopped off, waiting for Katrina.

"Wow." Katrina looked around. "This place is so pretty."

Nodding, Becky grinned, looking around also. "I come here a lot to fish or sometimes just to think. The boat ramp gets pretty busy during the weekends and during the day, but other than that you can find a spot along the river."

A large owl swooped down toward them then flew into a tree. Becky followed it with her eyes, staring at the beautiful creature. It's large round eyes stared back down at them.

"Oh, my God," Becky whispered. "Did you do that?"

"I heard him when we got here an d ask him to join us," Katrina whispered back.

"Tell it to fly to that tree," Becky whispered again, not wanting to alarm the owl. Suddenly the owl's head turned and it pushed off the branch, flying to the tree Becky had pointed to. "Holy crap!"

Katrina laughed, a proud smile on her face. "I can really communicate with them." She sighed, glancing at her surroundings. "I'm not crazy."

Soon they were surrounded by two deer, one buck, three rabbits, a possum, and a grumpy raccoon. Becky felt she was on an episode of the *Twilight Zone*. It was unreal.

Glancing at the two doe, Becky bit her lip. "Can I touch them?"

"Yes, but go slow," Katrina warned her.

Becky reached out, her fingers touching the softness of the doe. She couldn't believe she was surrounded by wild animals so close she could reach out and touch them all, and was actually stroking one like a pet. Her eyes went to the river.

"You think it works with fish?" Becky glanced back at Katrina.

"I can try." She walked to the edge of the water, the animals following.

The raccoon swiped at Becky's leg with its claws. "Hey, Ricky, watch it." She scolded the masked bandit who chattered at her.

Making it to the river's edge next to Katrina, Becky's eyes widened. The water rippled frantically as fish of all sizes swam near the edge around Katrina.

"Damn, what I wouldn't give for a fishing pole and worm right now." Becky laughed, kneeling down. A huge catfish swam in front of her.

"They don't like that." Katrina frowned.

"What?" Becky asked halfheartedly, her gaze returning to the fish. It was as if they were having a spawning party.

"Fishing." Katrina's voice was sad. "It hurts them."

"Oh." Guilt formed in Becky's chest as the large catfish stopped in front of her. "And the worm?"

"Hates it even more," Katrina replied, then laughed when Becky's head snapped up to her, shocked. "Kidding. I haven't connected with any worms yet, but I'd imagine getting stuck on a hook, dangling in the water, and then getting eaten isn't pleasant."

"Guess you have a point." Becky's eyebrows rose. On her hands and knees, she glanced over to see Ricky the Raccoon staring at her. "Is he going to bite me?"

"No." Katrina chuckled. "We are interrupting his 'garbage can' time though."

"Ah." Becky nodded in understanding, looking back at the large raccoon. "Sorry about that, Ricky my dude. Go ahead with your bad self."

The animal stared at her for a second before turning and wobbling away.

"Holy shit!" Becky sat back on her heels. "Did he just understand me?"

"Maybe." Katrina laughed.

"Well, this is awesome." Becky turned to look back at the lake. "Thank you for letting me be a part of thi— Oh. My. God!" Becky came face-to-face with a snake who had slithered up from the water. Her scream scared the fish, making them jump, splashing her with river water right in the face, soaking her.

Becky scrambled to her feet, turned to run, and smacked into a solid something. When she tried to move around it, hands grabbed her arms just as bright lights lit the area.

"Police!" voices shouted, filling the silence of the river. "Let the women go!"

Becky's head snapped up to see who she was fighting against only to see Sloan glaring down at her. "I really think you try to piss me off."

Becky opened her mouth to respond, but decided it wise to kept it closed. Seeing the look he threw her, she was certain she'd made the best decision.

******

Sloan and Blaze had stayed way back, wanting to see exactly what the women were up to. Parking their bikes off the road, they walked around the gate the women had ridden the scooter around. Both men scanned the area for possible danger.

Seeing the women, he watched a large owl swoop toward them then perch in a tree. He glanced at Blaze, who was also watching.

Sloan sent him a message so not to be heard by Katrina, and they stopped and watched. Soon animals edged toward the women and Sloan had to admit, he was amazed. Never had he seen anything like it.

Blaze glanced toward him, obviously stunned himself. A smile lifted the corner of Sloan's mouth when he saw Becky arguing with a raccoon. He watched as the women moved closer to the river. Becky got down on her hands and knees. Sloan's eyes followed her movement, stopping on her heart-shaped ass. With a silent curse, he pulled his gaze away to see the river rippling with activity.

A car door shut near the entrance and Sloan and Blaze turned. "We got company."

Sloan nodded, then headed toward the women. As soon as they arrived behind Becky and Katrina, the animals sensed them and scattered. Becky suddenly let out a scream, scaring the fish, who jumped, spraying water everywhere. Sloan caught Becky as she turned to run. He spotted the snake and realized what had Becky fleeing.

"Police!" two men shouted behind them as lights lit the area. "Let the women go!"

His eyes met Becky's. "I really think you try to piss me off." He then gave her a warning look as she started to speak. "Handcuff her," he ordered Blaze.

"I'm Sloan Murphy, VC Warrior," Sloan shouted without turning around. "I suggest you put those guns away."

Giving the officers a second, he turned his head to see that they had indeed put the guns away. Taking out his handcuffs, he looked back down at Becky. "Hands behind your back."

"Are you serious?" Becky whispered, staring up at him.

"Very serious. You broke the law." He turned her, then proceeded to handcuff her. When he turned her back around, his eyes went directly to her breasts underneath the white T-shirt. It was wet from the river. Her nipples poked toward him, making him want to—

"No, I did not." Becky gasped.

"Last I checked, trespassing is against the law." Sloan kept his eyes on hers and not any lower. "And the sign on the gate you went around clearly stated that the park closes at 9:00 p.m."

"Sorry, we've had some complaints of assault down here," one officer said.

Sloan raised his eyebrow at Becky, who looked away from his knowing look.

Do you need help?" one of the officers asked hopefully, his eyes raking over Becky's body. "We could take her to the station and book her for trespassing."

Sloan suddenly wanted to knock the fucker out. He knew his eyes had turned black because the cop took a step back. "I've got it," he warned, then dismissed him and his partner.

"She's not a vampire." The cop didn't heed Sloan's warning. "Which means—"

"Nothing." Sloan edged Becky behind him. "If you'd like to continue this bullshit, we can all go to the station and talk to the chief, who I can guarantee will take my side."

The cop looked like he was about to argue the matter more until he quickly looked down and let out a feminine scream. The snake that had scared Becky was slithering up his leg.

"Let's go," he told his partner as they headed out.

"Nice." Becky grinned at Katrina, who glared at the cops.

"Thank you," she said, but her glare continued, her eyes dark.

Sloan was also watching Katrina. She didn't trust cops, that much was evident. Becky pulled his attention away.

"Okay, they're gone." Becky turned, wiggling her fingers. "Can you take these things off me now?"

"No." Sloan took her arm and started to lead her out of the park with Blaze and Katrina, who was also still handcuffed.

"But what about my scooter?" Becky tried to stop, but he kept pulling her along. "It might get stolen."

"Good" was his only reply.

"Hey, no!" Becky finally stopped, jerking her arm out of his grip. "I'm not leaving my scooter."

"What the fuck is it with you and that fucking deathmobile." Sloan's temper flared.

"It's the only thing I own. It's mine," Becky finally said after a few minutes of silence.

And that small statement said so much about this proud woman. "Wait for us by the bikes," Sloan instructed Blaze as he stared at Becky. With a sigh, he turned her and removed the handcuffs, watching her rub her wrists.

When she continued to look at the ground, he used his knuckles to raise her face up to his. Unshed tears made her eyes glitter in the moonlight. She was a beautiful woman, a beautiful, proud woman.

"I can't leave it," Becky whispered. "If something happens and this job doesn't work out, then I would have no transportation. I refuse to live like that again."

Sloan stared down at her with an urge to pull her into his arms. She looked vulnerable, yet strong. Her head tilted at a slight angle in either a strong stance or waiting to be kissed, he wasn't sure which. Not really liking his thoughts, because he felt out of control, he cursed. "Ride the damn thing to where Blaze and Katrina are." He then turned to walk away. She was going to drive him insane.

"Sloan," Becky said, stopping him. "I don't try to piss you off." Her voice was strong and sure. "But it seems like that's all I do.

Sloan slowed, but didn't stop at her words. If he did stop, he would do exactly what he'd wanted to do since the moment he met her. He'd take her down by the river and fuck her, get her out of his system, as he did all women he found attractive. But he still had a little control over himself. He just didn't know how long that control was going to last. To play it safe, he walked away, knowing his feelings went much deeper than a basic attraction. As she passed on the damn scooter, he watched as she went back around the gate, but slowed so she could look at the sign. He couldn't help it, he chuckled. Damn, she was playing havoc with his emotions, and that was not good.

Chapter 16

Becky snuck her head inside Sloan's office and breathed a sigh of relief that he wasn't there. It had been awkward after she'd pulled up to them on her scooter. Katrina had hurried over and hopped on behind her. They'd turned out of the park, and Blaze and Sloan had surrounded them as they went down the road to her home.

They had sat on their bikes until they were safely inside, with a warning to stay put before they took off.

"Is he there?" Katrina whispered behind her.

"No," Becky whispered back, then rolled her eyes. Why the hell was she whispering?

"That's because he's behind you trying to get into his office," Sloan's voice boomed behind them.

Both women jumped with a scream and stumbled into the office. "You scared me."

"Good." Sloan passed them and headed to his desk. "Stop sneaking around. Though you are obviously good at that."

If she had a razor, she'd shave that damn cocked eyebrow right off his forehead. He sure was in a pissy mood. Seriously, what had they done that was so wrong? He should be thanking her for working with Katrina on her animal talking control thing. That wasn't even in her job description, but she was doing it. Well, that might be pushing it a little, but still.

Walking to the back, she angrily slapped her bag down on the desk, then turned only to find Sloan glaring at her. Okay, this had to stop.

"Why are you so angry with me?" She glared back, putting her hand on her hip. She didn't notice that more people had filed into the office.

"You should be thanking me."

"Thanking you?" Sloan laughed, not a funny "ha-ha" laugh, but a "you've lost your fucking mind" laugh. "What the hell would I be thanking you for? Riding that damn deathmobile at two in the morning, breaking into a park in the middle of the night, and almost getting one of my trainees arrested?"

"It's not a deathmobile. I didn't technically break anything to get into the park"—yeah, she was definitely pushing it—"and we wouldn't have gotten arrested because we would have gotten out of it."

"Oh, I'm sure you could have gotten out of it if you had got on your knees for one of the officers who seemed to take a liking to you," Sloan threw out with a sneer.

"Ah, eew." Becky narrowed her eyes at him. "That was disgusting."

"Lovers' spat?" Sid looked back and forth between them, eyes wide.

"Shut the fuck up," Sloan growled at the same time Becky voiced her "shut up" to Sid.

Glancing around, she realized they had an audience and decided to back down. This could wait. Turning around, she walked back to her desk and sat, then realized she didn't know what she should be doing. *Dammit!*

Hearing Sloan start to talk, she slowly swiveled her chair around to listen and felt really awkward. Her eyes met Katrina's, who stared at her with a sad expression. Becky just shrugged then went back to listening.

"We found another abandoned building on Fifth Street last night. So any patrols in that area need to keep an eye on that building. We found old blood, though we're not sure how old, but it's definitely been used for something," Sloan said then looked around. "Where's Jill and Adam?"

"They're on their way," Steve said, glancing at his phone.

"Sorry." Jill ran in with Adam following her. "What's up?"

"You three are going to be helping with the trainees." Sloan didn't hesitate to throw out that order. "Seems we got some real wannabe badasses not playing nice with the other trainees."

Everyone's eyes went to Katrina.

"Sweet!" Jill smiled, rubbing her hands together.

"I've cleared your schedules so you're free," Sloan added, his voice grumpy. "You are Blaze and Jax's until they say otherwise."

"I mean, are we just kicking ass and taking names or are we helping them?" Steve stood all proud of being asked to help the trainees.

"They have been singling Katrina out. They think she's getting special treatment by whoring herself out to the Warriors." Sloan's blunt explanation rang through the room.

"Who the fuck has been saying that?" Steve growled, his eyes narrowing.

Becky could see Katrina shift from foot to foot, obviously not liking being the center of attention.

"Those thoughts may change once they find out what power she possesses." Sloan glanced toward Becky, then away. "What Blaze and I witnessed last night was pretty amazing. I've never seen anything like it."

"Are you freaking kidding me? You already have a power? Where the fuck is my power is what I want to know?" Steve deflated before everyone's eyes. He looked toward Katrina. "What power do you have?"

When Katrina just shrugged, Becky wanted to urge her to speak about it. Sloan was right about one thing: it was absolutely amazing what she could do.

"Since Becky witnessed it up close and personal, why don't you explain what you saw." Sloan's peered at her as if daring her to stand up and speak.

Oh, she was the champ of truth or dare. Did he think because he was being an ass she was going to sit around with her thumb up her ass and stay quiet? Pfft, not likely. Standing, she gave him a "really?" smirk.

Heading toward Katrina, she smiled genuinely. "This beautiful woman has a unique gift of communicating with animals."

"What do you mean?" Jared's eyes narrowed in disbelief. "Animals talk to her?"

"Actually, I'm not sure." She looked toward Katrina. "Do they?"

"No, not really," Katrina replied, looking only at Becky. "We just... understand each other."

"Not like Dr. Dolittle?" Sid smirked. "Because that would be cool."

Becky saw a flash of unease pass across Katrina's face, and it pissed her off. "Well, I think when she has a snake bite you on the ass, that will be cool." She frowned at Sid. "It's something that's hard to explain. You just have to see it."

"*Dr. Dolittle* was a great movie," Steve added thoughtfully. "The drunk monkey was the shit."

"The bear, what was his name, Archie?" Adam laughed. "He was the best."

"No way," Jill broke in. "The raccoon made that movie."

Becky looked over at Sloan with a smirk. "They saw the movie."

He narrowed his eyes at her before looking at Katrina. "Do you think you can do a demonstration?"

"Yes," Katrina replied, glancing at Blaze.

Becky also looked toward Blaze, who hadn't taken his eyes off Katrina until he glanced at his watch.

"Why don't we head to the warehouse for the demonstration. All the trainees will be showing up for the morning training." Blaze once again looked toward Katrina.

"Sounds perfect." Sloan stood as everyone headed out the door.

Figuring this was a "Warrior" thing, Becky turned and headed toward her desk, feeling a little left out. But she was just the secretary, what did she expect?

"Are you coming?" Sloan's voice echoed in the empty room. When Becky turned around, her face a mask of confusion, her eyes landed on Sloan, who stood by the door. "You're the one who took her out last night to practice."

"I thought I was in trouble for that," Becky replied, but headed toward him, excited to be included.

"You are." Sloan's voice was stern, but his eyes no longer looked angry. "I'm just letting your indiscretions build up for one punishment."

"Which is?" Becky asked, following him outside to his motorcycle.

Sloan climbed on his bike, making him almost eye level with her. "Get on."

Becky actually looked at his lap, thinking, if only. Her eyes shot to his to see him staring at her, and she knew he was aware of exactly what she was thinking. Quickly, she jumped on the back of the bike, her arms held tightly to her sides. Just her legs and crotch touching him was way too much. If she wrapped her arms around him, there was no telling what the hell she would do. Grabbing his junk was a total possibility. Holy hell, she was a mess.

"You need to hold on," he said over the hum of the bike.

"I'm good." Becky cringed, feeling around for something to hold on to other than him.

He reached backward with both hands and found hers. He wrapped her arms around him before taking off. My God, he was built. The feeling of his powerful, masculine stature beneath her fingertips was almost more than she could stand. Fighting to keep her fingers still, she bit her lip and held on. Maybe if she thought of an old wrinkly man, she could fight the urge to actually grab his junk. Yes, she was that close to losing control. Was she that desperate for a man? Apparently, yes, she was.

The ride was short, but not short enough that she wasn't holding on to him with her front smashed to his back by the time they got to where they were going. Oh, no. She was plastered to him within seconds of the ride. She didn't know how that happened, she lied to herself. Yeah, she did, and it could possibly take a pry bar to pry her ass off him.

Once they stopped, it took everything she had to release him, but she did take a long whiff because damn, he smelled good. He helped her off the bike. She noticed his eyes were black before he quickly looked away from her as he headed toward everyone else. And yes, her eyes went directly to his ass. She was such a slut.

Chapter 17

Katrina was so nervous she wanted to vomit. Everyone stared at her and the trainees were showing up but staying outside instead of going in. Her eyes searched around, finding Becky, who offered her a reassuring nod. She had no idea what to do. This stuff just happened. She'd never really tried to call upon it until last night. Her breathing sped up, which was especially weird as she was a vampire. She hadn't had a panic attack since being turned and she felt one coming on. Blaze stood with his arms crossed just watching her, which honestly was driving her nuts. That was all he did, watch her, constantly.

Gulping, she felt as if her throat was closing. Oh, God. She really was going to have a panic attack in front of everybody.

"Hey, you okay?" Becky moved closer to her and whispered.

Shaking her head, Katrina looked over at Becky and wished she was more like her, like anyone else other than herself.

"You've got this, Katrina," Becky urged her.

"I don't know what to do," Katrina replied honestly.

"Do the same thing you did last night." Becky glanced around before looking back at Katrina. "This is your chance. Take it."

Katrina closed her eyes tightly, letting her mind clear. Opening them, she felt a little better and wanted to hug Becky. Hearing birds in the trees that surrounded the warehouse, she called upon them. As one, the birds flew out of the trees and began to circle above them. More birds of different kinds appeared. She watched along with everyone else as they circled above them.

"Can you tell them not to shit on us?" Steve looked up, wary but impressed. "Because as cool as this shit is right now, shit being the key word, I don't want to be pooped on."

Katrina actually grinned, her eyes going toward the trainees. The birds began in an organized fashion to scatter and went back to the trees. This time a large buck came walking across the parking lot, his eyes on her and her alone. She made sure to let the huge animal know he was safe. He walked straight up to her, snorted, and pawed the concrete pavement.

"Hello, Buck." Katrina smiled and reached out to touch the side of his massive head. "I see you found me."

"I'll be damned." Sid's tone was one of shocked awe.

"I wouldn't mind having that head on my wall. Look at the rack on that son of a bitch." Ben's voice reached her, and her temper, which rarely reared its ugly head, rose like a beast.

Katrina's gaze snapped toward him. The buck became agitated, stomping and snorting, but Katrina kept her hand on him. "You ever harm him, I'll kill you." Her words shocked not only her, but everyone present.

"I didn't think trainees were supposed to threaten each other" was Ben's sarcastic reply.

Looking back toward the trees, a handful of birds flew out and over Ben. A large white pile of shit hit him on the head as more followed.

"Son of a bitch!" Ben wiped bird shit off his forehead, heading toward Katrina, but Blaze stepped in front of her.

"Go get cleaned up," Blaze warned Ben with a nod.

Katrina peeked around Blaze to see Ben give her one last glare. Then she turned to look at Becky. "That was me."

Becky laughed, then reached out to hug Katrina. "Hang with me, friend. I'll teach you everything you need to know about being a righteous bitch."

"Thank you." Katrina touched Becky's arm.

"For what? I didn't do anything," Becky replied, then grinned. "This was all you."

Katrina watched her go, then looked up toward Blaze, who still stood beside her.

"You need to watch your back," Blaze warned.

Nodding, Katrina turned back to Buck. "Go, and stay out of sight." She watched as he turned and headed to where he had come from.

"Why didn't you tell me about this?" Blaze watched the large buck disappear before he looked down at her.

"Because I didn't want to be looked at as odd, at least any more than I already am," Katrina answered honestly.

"Well, you are odd," Steve teased, hearing the conversation. "We all are, but dammit, I'm jealous as hell. When in the fuck am I going to get my superpowers? Seriously, your power is cool. Who wouldn't want to have a flock of birds on command to shit on people who piss you off."

"You with that power would not be good." Adam chuckled as he walked past them.

"I'd be like Tarzan and my best friend would be a monkey, not an asshole vampire," Steve shot back at Adam, who flipped him off as he headed into the warehouse.

"Well played." Jill passed Katrina with a proud grin.

"Thanks," Katrina replied, staring at the warehouse, her nerves getting worse, not better.

Blaze headed toward the warehouse, but stopped and turned. "You training today?"

Katrina nodded, then followed up to the door and walked inside. Everyone was staring at her, the oddball. She wished she were used to it, but she wasn't. The door opened behind her and she moved out of the way.

"Sorry I missed the show." Jax walked in, looking down at Katrina. "You'll have to do an encore after training."

He didn't even give her a chance to respond before he walked out onto the mats, yelling at the trainees to get running. Not looking at Blaze as she passed him, she hit the mats and took off running, wishing she could go back to being the girl in the corner.

******

Blaze watched Katrina pass him and he knew she hated the attention. He still couldn't believe that she could control animals. Steve was right; it was awesome, and it could come in great use to them in the future. Walking out onto the mats, he crossed his arms and observed how the other trainees acted toward Katrina. She still ran alone, while others were in groups. His eyes met Jill's and he gave her a nod.

Jill took off and began running next to Katrina. Next his eyes met Adam and then Steve's. With another nod, they took off both running next to Ben and his group.

"What's the plan?" Jax walked up to Blaze.

"I say we just do what we always do and integrate Jill, Adam, and Steve wherever we see fit," Blaze replied, then frowned when Ben sped up so he was running directly behind Katrina, then beside her.

"No animals in here, kiss ass." Even though Ben spoke low, Blaze and Jax heard him, and so did Jill.

Blaze watched as Jill's hand rose and a broom used to sweep the mats shot out, tripping Ben, who did a stomach slide on the mats, his skin skidding on the mat making a loud noise.

"No, but there're assholes, jerk." Jill smirked as she and Katrina passed. Some of the trainees laughed, but Adam and Steve laughed the loudest.

Steve slowed and continued to run in place, but bent down, looking at Ben who cursed before pushing himself back up. "Hurts, don't it?" Steve laughed again before taking off.

"Don't worry," Jill told Katrina as they passed Blaze and Jax. "Soon you'll be taking care of assholes like him. It took me a while to find myself too."

Blaze grinned, watching Ben picking himself off the ground. The kid was either going to learn or get his ass handed to him. Honestly he hoped he learned, because the guy had potential, but he let his arrogance get in the way and that was going to be his downfall.

"And maybe we won't have to do anything." Jax chuckled, shaking his head before walking to the middle of the mat. "Okay, partner up."

Making sure Ben and Adam were partners, Blaze put Steve with another potential asshole who didn't like to take orders.

"During your training you are going to get hit, and if you become a Warrior, you will definitely get hit." Blaze walked toward Jax and stood across from him. "Your first goal is to not get hit, but if and when you do, your survival is going to depend on how you react."

Jax and Blaze dropped into a fighting stance.

"What I want you to do with your partner is to go back and forth doing your best to touch their face with just your fingers." They demonstrated going back and forth with each other. "Use control, keep focused."

Blaze walked around helping, as did Jax. His eyes flicked to Jill and Katrina. They worked well together.

"Okay, good." Jax stopped them. "The first person to get touched, stop and sit on the mat. The other person remain standing. This teaches humility, because no one wants to sit down. No one wants to be bested, but we also get to see who has the bad attitude and shows their ass in anger. So the person who gets touched better sit their ass down and fast."

Again everyone started. Ben was the first to sit down and he didn't look happy about it. Soon all action had stopped.

"Everyone stand," Jax commanded. "Now that you have the hang of it, you will be dodging punches. Continue until we say stop."

Stepping back, Blaze knew what was coming, and he was right. Fights broke out and it wasn't until Adam picked up Ben and slammed him to the mat that Jax stopped them.

"When in a fight, never become angry because the angry fighter will lose 99.9 percent of the time." Jax walked up to Adam. "Did you become angry? Is that why you slammed him?"

Calm and cool, Adam replied, "No, total opposite. He became angry because he couldn't touch me, and I believe it wasn't until I touched his face with my fist for the sixth time that he became enraged and started throwing haymakers without thought. When I warned him to calm down, he became angrier, so I felt it was time to stop, and I stopped it by sitting his ass down."

"Who became angry?" Blaze asked, looking around.

More than half the trainees raised their hands.

"Okay, switch partners," Jax ordered. "Jill, you replace Adam. Steve, you go with Katrina and, Adam, find some poor fucker to go with."

Once everyone had their partners, Jax ordered them to go.

"Don't pull your punches," Steve told Katrina. "You could have hit me with that one."

Blaze had been watching and Steve was right. Katrina could have made definite contact on her last punch, but had pulled it.

"Do you want to become a Warrior or not?" Blaze narrowed his eyes at Katrina.

"Yes," she replied, in her usual soft voice.

"Then fucking act like it and punch him when you have the chance." Blaze growled. "If not, sit your ass down. Only 100 percent in here. If you can't give that, then leave."

Katrina frowned, then turned and punched Steve in the nose, hard.

"Motherfucker." Steve grabbed his nose. "Dammit, Katrina. I wasn't ready."

"Good job." Blaze gave her an approving nod. "And what is the first lesson any trainee learns, Steve?"

"Be ready for anything," Steve grumbled, his eyes watering as he held his nose.

Blaze turned to leave, but saw Katrina giving Steve *that* look and knew what was coming before she even opened her mouth. "Don't you fucking apologize."

Katrina snapped her mouth closed. When she and Steve began again, Blaze looked down at Jill and cringed when she took a hard hit. Damn good thing Slade wasn't around. Blaze looked at Jax, who raised an eyebrow then went back to watching Jill and Ben go at it.

It was as if Jill and Ben were trading blows. Jill would deliver a good one that would knock Ben back a few steps. He'd then move his neck back and forth before they'd start again. Jill then dodged one, but took a hit when Ben came around with the other hand. Blaze knew that had hurt, but Jill just spat blood and continued.

"Stop!" Jax ordered, and threw them an approving nod. "Much better. Take five and grab something to drink, then back on the mat."

Blaze kept an eye on Ben as he walked away from Jill without shaking her hand. She just shrugged it off until Ben opened his mouth with his buddies.

"She's nothing." Ben's voice carried. "Got a few shots in, but she hits like a girl."

Shaking his head, Blaze watched Jill's calm control crack. Her hands shot up, and so did Ben. As Ben did some hang time in the air, Jill pulled him closer to her. Then with a shove, Ben shot through the air and through the wall. Jill followed him outside through the hole.

"How's that for a girl, dickhead?" Jill yelled as she headed toward the hole that bright sunlight shone through.

"Shit!" Blaze headed after her with Jax, the rest of the group close on his heels. Glancing over, he saw Katrina also rushing toward the hole with a large grin on her face. She looked absolutely beautiful. "Shit!" Blaze said again, this time with a little more heat.

Chapter 18

Waiting for Sloan, Becky leaned against his motorcycle. What she really wanted to do was go inside the warehouse to watch what was going on, but she didn't know if that was top secret stuff. She hadn't been able to even ask him because he had been on the phone and then Damon and Duncan had been there talking to him. She had never in her life seen a busier man.

Grabbing her phone, she checked her messages. One from her son saying calculus sucked, but he was sitting next to some hot chick so that made it much better. Becky rolled her eyes with a grin. To Frankie, a hot chick made everything much better. She missed him so much, but loved him enough to let him go find himself and his own life. She was here for him and always would be. Though she did threaten him that Christmas was her time and his ass better be home or she'd visit him at least every other weekend.

A loud noise jerked her out of her thoughts and as she looked up, she watched a body fly through the warehouse wall and roll across the concrete parking lot. Sloan was in front of her before she knew what was happening. She peeked around him to see Jill stomping through the hole with everyone following.

"Ah, damn." Sloan started to walk away, but stopped. "Stay here," he ordered, then took off with Damon and Duncan.

She technically listened to him; actually no, she didn't. She moved close enough so she could hear what was going on. Her gaze landed on Katrina, who glanced her way. Becky opened her eyes wide in question, but Katrina just gave her an amused grin.

"What in the hell is it with you and walls?" Sloan yelled at Jill. Jill didn't even flinch. Becky did, but Jill stood strong.

"Sometimes I don't know my own power," Jill replied to Sloan's question, though it was obviously directed toward Ben, who was picking himself off the ground. "Though it's funny that I apparently hit like a girl, like that's a bad thing."

"If you weren't a woman…." Ben headed toward her, but Sloan stepped in front of him.

"Go ahead, bitch!" Jill spread her arms wide. "Take your best shot."

"Do I need to toss you out of this program?" Sloan shouted, his eyes narrowing on Ben. "Can't you just keep you fucking mouth shut and train?"

"She's the one who threw me through a wall." Ben pointed around Sloan to Jill.

"Damn straight I did and I'll do it again." Jill took a step forward.

"Jill, get to my office," Sloan ordered without even turning around to look at her. When she didn't move, Sloan roared, "Now!"

Once Jill had left and without a smartass comment, which Becky was sure was a miracle, Sloan once again focused on Ben. "This is it," Sloan said, his voice even and stern. "One more fucking thing with you and you're out. Get the fucking chip off your shoulder where women are concerned and train. You understand me?"

"Yes, sir." Ben nodded, appearing to have calmed down.

Sloan looked at Jax and Blaze. "They can spend the rest of their morning cleaning this shit up."

When moans and bitching started, Becky watched Sloan stop as he headed toward her and turn back to everyone. "Anyone who has a problem with that can fucking leave."

Becky wasn't surprised that no one admitted having a problem because she was almost ready to start helping. Sloan Murphy was an intimidating man and when he said something, you'd better get your ass in gear.

Sloan passed her and mounted his bike, then looked at her. "You coming?"

Not saying a word, Becky hopped on the back. Thinking, *screw it,* she wrapped her arms around him. The perks of a secretary. She grinned.

While Becky enjoyed the short ride back to the compound, she noticed a blue sedan with dark tinted windows keeping pace with them. As Sloan turned into the compound, she watched as the sedan slowed to a complete stop. She was about to say something to Sloan when it took off.

He helped her off the bike, then headed inside with her following. She glanced over her shoulder, but the car was no longer in view. Maybe someone was lost. She shrugged it off and walked into the office where Jill sat in front of Sloan's desk. Becky headed to her desk, wishing she had something to do, but she hadn't had time to ask.

"Sorry about the wall." Jill started the conversation. "I'll pay for it."

"Yes, you will," Sloan's replied. "Jill, you need to stop putting people through walls, my walls."

Becky had pulled out her phone so she looked busy, but she couldn't help overhear since she was right there.

"Then these assholes need to learn to stop acting like women don't belong. You know that pisses me off, Sloan," Jill shot back. "It's hard being a woman in a man's world and this is definitely a man's world within the VC. A woman has to fight for every tiny scrap of respect, and it's not right."

Becky wanted so badly to turn around during the silence to see Sloan's reaction. She felt for both Jill and Katrina. She couldn't imagine trying to compete for a position with these men. Jill was right. It wasn't fair.

"We work just as hard, bleed just as much, hurt just the same, yet when we get the upper hand, we get called into your office." Jill's voice rose and sounded hurt, at least to Becky's ears. "With all due respect, it's bullshit. Where is that asshole?"

"Cleaning up the mess you both made." Sloan's voice was even. Becky couldn't tell anything from it. Sloan was a puzzle that gave nothing away. Dammit, she wished she could turn around, but she needed to mind her own business and snoop without a visual.

"Still bullshit that he's there and I'm here," Jill muttered, but Becky heard her loud and clear. She cringed, waiting for Sloan's response.

"Why did you slam him through the wall?" Sloan asked.

Again there was silence and Becky leaned back in her chair to make sure she heard everything. The chair tilted dangerously, making her jerk, trying not to fall over. Rolling her eyes at herself, she decided she would never make a good detective.

Jill finally sighed. "We were doing a drill and he said I hit like a girl."

"Are you fucking kidding me?" Sloan roared. Becky almost dropped her phone, but grabbed it quickly. "You threw a man through a wall because he said you hit like a girl?"

"Yeah, I did." Jill's voice also rose, but she had nothing on Sloan. "Like any single one of those warriors I know so well, you included, wouldn't do the same."

Again silence. Becky stared at her phone, but didn't see it. She was waiting to see what Sloan was going to say. She actually felt sorry for him. The shit he must put up with on a daily basis was enough to drive anyone insane, even a strong man as him.

"If I put you in a position of authority, you are going to have to try to keep your ass calm, Jill." Sloan finally spoke. "I don't do anything without thinking it through, and putting you with the trainees is a benefit to them and me, but not if you're going to take them out if they look at you wrong."

"It wasn't just that." Jill snorted, but her voice had calmed. "I just get sick of guys thinking they're the shit and that women belong behind a desk typing a letter or some shit. No offense, Becky."

Shit, did they know she'd been listening? Well, of course they did—she was in the same room. She'd never make a good Warrior either. Yep, scratch detective and Warrior off her possible job opportunities. "None taken," she replied, still not turning around.

"You have no idea what it's like, Sloan." Defeat laced Jill's words, surprising Becky. She'd heard a lot about Jill and from just the short time she had known her, she seemed like one hell of a strong woman. Then again, strong women broke sometimes; she should know. She did.

"No, I guess I don't," Sloan finally admitted. "Just try to let shit roll off you, Jill. And yes, I would tell the other Warriors the same thing."

"Okay, I'll try," Jill agreed. "So how much do you think that wall is going to be?"

Becky grinned at the question. Having that taken out of your paycheck would suck since it was a big hole. Poor Jill. Again there was silence. That was one thing she had learned about Sloan. He never answered on a whim. He thought every response through, even if it drove the person waiting for the answer crazy.

"I've got it, but don't let it happen again." Sloan's voice was low. "Do you know how many walls I've fixed because of you?"

"No, I've lost count," Jill replied, and Becky could hear the smile in her voice.

"Get the fuck out of my office," Sloan ordered. "Go help clean up that mess. I'll have someone there today to fix it."

Thinking it was over, Becky turned to see Jill lean down and hug Sloan. Sloan sat stoic at his desk, staring down. He definitely wasn't used to hugs, that was evident. He looked like a terrified statue. A strange sadness enveloped her as she watched Sloan's uncomfortable reaction to being touched with care.

"Thanks, and I'm sorry." Jill straightened and headed for the door. "But do you think you could bring in trainees who aren't total assholes?"

"Don't push me, Jill," Sloan warned. "Slade still at the hospital?"

"Yeah, he should be back soon." Jill held the door while she answered. "Why, do you need him?"

"Yes, to keep your ass in line," Sloan replied, looking down at his phone.

"Pfft!" was Jill's only reply before she left with a grin spreading across her face.

Once the door shut, Becky glanced at Sloan, who remained staring at his phone. She had a sudden overwhelming urge to hug him and even took a step toward him before he looked up at her. It stopped her cold. What the hell was she doing?

"Ah, you want me to call some construction people and get some prices?" Becky asked, clearing her shaky throat. Holy shit, she'd almost hugged the crap out of her boss.

"I'm trying to find the last one Sid organized. They did a good job, but I can't find the number." Sloan frowned, his eyes going back to his phone. "Maybe Sid called them, not me."

"Let me take care of it." Becky actually grabbed his phone and put it facedown. "You're paying me to pretty much sit around, listen to conversations that aren't my business, ride on the back of your motorcycle, which is a big perk by the way, and I feel like I'm taking advantage of you. Let me do the work."

Sloan's eyes darkened slightly. "You like riding?"

"Absolutely." Becky grinned, but watched his eyes. They were amazing when they changed colors like that. "When Frankie was younger, we use to ride dirt bikes all the time."

Sloan smiled his head tilting as he studied her. "Yeah, I can definitely see you riding dirt bikes."

"I was pretty fearless," she bragged, then sighed. "I really miss those days."

"Too old now?" he teased with a raised eyebrow.

"Hell no. Thirty… ah, something is not too old. I still got it." She put her hand on her hip, looking offended, but she wasn't. She knew he was teasing her and she liked it. Plus, age was just a number, and she would beat that into her brain when the big four-oh came rolling around.

He continued to stare at her to the point she started feeling hot, everywhere. The man had the stare down, that was for damn sure.

"Now, give me Sid's number so I can take some of this off your shoulders. That is why you hired me, isn't it?" She broke the silence before she went up in flames.

Finally, he looked away and picked up his phone. He rattled off Sid's number as well as the other Warriors', which she quickly wrote down. Heading back to her desk, she picked up her phone, wishing she had just gone ahead and hugged him to get it over with. She knew herself well and she knew a hug was coming. Deep down, she hoped it led to something more than a hug.

Chapter 19

It took two days for the contactors to finish the wall. Becky drove to the warehouse with the check to pay them on her way home. Sloan had been gone since the previous day for meetings and had left her in charge with distinct instructions on what needed to be done. The man had his shit together, that was for sure. She didn't know how he did it.

Turning into the warehouse, the parking lot was empty other than the workers and their vehicles. Training didn't start for another hour. They had pushed it back so the workers could finish.

Parking, she got out of the car with the check. Glancing at it, she noticed how neat and precise Sloan's handwriting was. Her thumb rubbed against his signature, then she laughed at herself. She was so pathetic. She hadn't seen him for twenty-four hours and she missed him. How she could become so attracted to someone so fast, especially after her exhausting failed marriage and her promise to herself to be a crazy cat lady—even though she was allergic to them—or a lesbian, was beyond her. Neither of those options appealed to her anymore, and that was scary because before meeting Sloan Murphy, they did appeal to her very much, runny nose and all.

"Looks good." She stared at the wall as she walked up to Don Baker of Baker's Construction. "You finished?"

"We sure are," Don replied with a proud smile. "Just cleaning up. Come on in and look at the inside before we leave."

Becky followed him inside to check their work and all looked good. "You guys do a wonderful job."

Don chuckled. "Well, we've gotten a lot of experience with replacing walls with this group."

"I bet you have." Becky laughed in agreement, handing him the check. "And I'm sure you'll be hearing from us again."

"I count on it." Don stared at their work with pride.

"Looks good, Don." Sloan had snuck in on them. He stuck his hand out to shake Don's hand.

Becky watched Sloan's hand swallow the other man's, who wasn't small by any means. What in the hell was it about a man's hands? Jerking her gaze away, she cursed at herself to get a grip.

"Did Becky get you your check?" Sloan said, breaking into Becky's stupid "man hand" thoughts.

"Yes, sir." Don raised the check. "You got a good worker there. I thought a few times to try to sway her to leave you and come work for me. She had my boys busting ass to get this done. Very impressive."

"Ah, now, Don, I was nice to those boys and even brought them lunch yesterday," Becky teased. "I wasn't busting anyone's ass, but I may have bribed them with some fried chicken."

"Well, I don't know what the hell you did, but it worked." Don laughed, looking back at the wall. "Never saw them work that hard on a project. You sure you're happy here?"

Becky glanced up at Sloan who looked down at her with what appeared to be pride, but that couldn't be right. "I think I'll stay." She turned her attention back to Don. "But thanks for the endorsement here today. That will come in handy during raise time."

"Anytime." Don gave a nod then headed toward his workers, who kept glancing at Becky.

"Looks like you won a few hearts here," Sloan said, his voice tight.

Becky glanced up at him. His eyes were narrowed toward the men. "Nah, it was the fried chicken. I make a mean fried bird." She chuckled, a little confused about his sudden change of mood. "Okay, I'm off to get your tux. You need me to do anything else? Some food maybe? I'm sure you haven't eaten anything. I can stop and pick something up real quick."

Sloan finally stopped glaring at the workers to look down at her. "They get home-cooked fried chicken and I get something quick from a fast-food joint?" He frowned.

"Hey, you got your wall fixed in record time." She laughed, giving him a shove as she passed. "I'll fix you some fried chicken if it stops you pouting."

"I don't pout." Sloan growled as he followed her outside, walking her to her car.

Don and his workers were just pulling out, but there was a car left by the entrance that they had just passed. Neither paid much attention to it. "Oh, I think that was definitely a pout," she teased, but seeing the look on his face warned her something was definitely wrong. Before she could say anything else, she was in his arms as a loud explosion rocked them off their feet. Sloan shielded her with his body as they hit the ground hard.

Her ears roared, her vision was fuzzy, and she couldn't catch her breath. Even during all that, her head turned to see Don and his men running toward them screaming something. Something blue caught her eye, the sedan from the other day, and then it was gone as Sloan's face appeared in front of her. His mouth moved, but all she could hear was the annoying roar in her ears.

******

Sloan knew she was hurt. Motherfucker! Quickly grabbing his phone, he put it to his ear. "Get everyone to the warehouse now, and bring Slade!" he ordered into the phone before tossing it to the ground. His eyes never left Becky, who lay underneath him, her eyes appearing unfocused.

"We called an ambulance," Don yelled. "You better move. It might blow up again."

Turning slightly, Sloan watched the parked car they had passed burn, the heat so intense he felt it heating the bottom of his boots. He looked back down at Becky.

"Becky?" Sloan leaned into her vision again. "We need to move. Can I pick you up? Where are you hurt?"

She just stared at his lips for a few minutes before even attempting to answer. "I'm okay," she finally managed. Her hearing was probably fucked from the explosion.

"The hell you are." Sloan moved off her. Even though he had taken his weight off her, he shielded her from harm. "But I have to move you away from this."

When she didn't answer, but just lay there staring at him, worry pulsed through him. He wished to hell Slade would get there. Kneeling, he bent down and gently picked her up. He slowed when she grimaced, but continued. Even for him the heat was intense. He knew he had some damage because his back was hurting like a son of a bitch, but he would heal. Becky was his only concern.

Motorcycles and pounding feet hitting the pavement indicated that his team had arrived. "Where's Slade?" he shouted, not once taking his eyes off her.

"Jesus, Sloan." Duncan stopped beside him, his eyes on Sloan's back. "You've got metal in your back."

Sloan laid Becky down, ignoring Duncan and the pain in his back. Slade slid in on his knees and began checking Becky, who kept pointing at Sloan.

"What is it?" Sloan leaned down, wondering why she kept pointing.

"She wants me to check you first." Slade touched her neck with his hands, but she kept pushing him away.

"I'm fine," she said loudly. "You're bleeding."

Sloan knelt down, grabbing her hands so Slade to could finish looking her over. "As soon as he's done checking you, he can check me over." Sloan leaned down, trying to calm her. "I'm vampire, you're not."

That seemed to calm her, but he kept her small hands in his. "She okay?"

"I think so, but she's obviously lost some hearing, which should come back." Slade's exam moved down to her stomach. He pushed into her skin while watching her face. "How close were you?" When Sloan didn't respond, Slade looked up at him.

"A few steps away," Sloan replied, anger forcing the words out.

"I think we need to get you both to the hospital." Slade leaned back so he could look around at Sloan's back. "We need to make sure nothing is broken that could heal badly with you, and she should really get a CAT scan."

"No." Becky must have either gotten some hearing back or she was a damn good lip-reader. "I don't have insurance. I'm fine." She went to sit up, but Slade stopped her.

"She needs to go," Slade told Sloan. "That was a hell of a blast at close range."

The ambulance had arrived, as did the police. Sloan had to get his anger in check. He would find whoever was responsible for, but not today. Duncan and Damon stood close to him waiting for orders, while the rest looked for evidence. They all knew their jobs; he didn't have to worry about that. The paramedics were waiting for Slade's orders and Slade was waiting for Sloan's.

Looking down at Becky's pale face, he knew she needed to go and by the stares he was getting at his back, so did he, and that pissed him off. Whoever had done this could have killed her, possibly him, but he was one hard son of a bitch to kill.

"Make sure no one goes near that car until you Warriors have checked it over. After that, the police can do what they want," Sloan ordered those around him, knowing that the rest would get word. "Whoever is behind this will be caught by us." He looked them each in the eye.

Duncan, who had received a phone call and had walked away, returned to the group, his face a mask of rage.

"Looks like we weren't the only ones hit." Duncan cursed, his eyes going back to the car and then to Sloan. "Other training centers in a hundred-mile radius were also hit."

"Looks like someone doesn't want more Warriors running about kicking ass," Sid hissed.

"Was anyone hurt?" Sloan asked, his eyes narrowing when one of the paramedics made Becky moan in pain. Walking over, he knocked the guy out of the way and lifted Becky in his arms before he repeated his question to Duncan.

"No, but one building was destroyed." Duncan glanced at the car that was still burning, but the fire department was working on getting it under control. "The rest were like this. A car near the building. Like a warning."

Sloan nodded, then turned and headed to the ambulance with Becky in his arms. The paramedics had to run to get the stretcher back in place before he arrived with Becky.

"Put me down, Sloan." Becky frowned up at him. "You're hurt."

Sloan glanced at her. "Are you calling me weak?"

"No, but you have stuff sticking out of your back." Becky's worried voice did something to him, something he hadn't felt in such a long time. "Slade, tell him to put me down."

"I did. He won't listen." Slade sneered, the doctor in him not liking what he was seeing.

"Don't make my redhead 'tude come out," Becky warned Sloan, then cringed.

Sloan slowed. "Are you okay?"

"Yes," she replied, but he knew she was lying. "And I don't have insurance. I can't afford to go to the hospital. I'll be fine. Lost my hearing for a minute, but it's coming back already."

Quickening his steps, Sloan carried her into the ambulance and laid her gently on the stretcher. He then turned to the paramedics as Slade climbed in.

"What the fuck are we waiting for?" Sloan cursed, not in the mood to fuck around.

Slade banged his fist on the wall of the ambulance twice. The ambulance sirens started just as they began to move.

Becky turned, looking up at Sloan. "Do vampires have a high pain tolerance?"

"No." A slow smile spread across his face. "I'm just trying to impress you."

"Well, it's working." Becky grinned back. "Here I am with a little hearing loss lying on the stretcher and you have glass and metal sticking out of your back."

"Just part of the job," Sloan replied, then glanced at Slade who stared at him with an odd expression. He sent the doc a silent message, warning him if this conversation left the ambulance, he would be a dead man.

Chapter 20

Becky was done with the poking, testing, and the rest of the crap that went along with being in the emergency room. Her hearing was almost back to normal. She was just a little sore from Sloan falling on her. More than anything, she was bored to death and worried about Sloan.

He had stayed with her, along with some of the Warriors, until Slade had collected him. She was since alone. She sat up in the uncomfortable bed listening to the conversations going on around her. She couldn't see anything because the curtains were closed, but she could see feet walking back and forth.

No one had been in for the last half an hour and she was ready to get dressed and find out what was going on with Sloan. Glancing down at the IV port they put in the top of her hand, she frowned. Ripping the tape off, the pulled it out and cursed. "Damn, that hurts." As soon as it left her hand, blood squirted everywhere. "Ah, shit!" She frantically reached around to find something to stop the blood. Coming up empty, she used her bedsheet. Using that to put pressure on the small hole, she looked for her clothes.

Once the bleeding had stopped, she hopped out of the bed, waiting for a second to make sure she really was okay and not going to fall flat on her face. Taking a step, then another toward the chair with her clothes, she felt triumphant as she hurried and dressed.

Peeking out the curtains, she glanced around. If she was going to make a break for it, now was the time. It was clear. Quickly she walked out, then slowed, wondering where the hell Sloan was. Turning up another hallway, she watched Slade walk out of a room. She pushed herself against the wall, then peeked to make sure he was gone and saw the Warriors standing around at the end of the hallway, talking. Katrina spotted her. Putting her finger to her lips, Becky warned Katrina to shush, then pointed toward the room Slade had exited and mouthed "Sloan." Katrina glanced around at the Warriors, then nodded.

With a sneakiness that would make the Warriors proud, she crossed the hallway to the wall and plastered herself against it. Easing herself along, she reached out, grabbed the knob, and snuck into Sloan Murphy's room. With a satisfied smile, she turned, her eyes falling on Sloan's back.

"Oh, my God!" Her hand went to her mouth in shock.

Sloan lay on his stomach on a bed. He pushed himself up to see her. "What in the hell are you doing up?"

"Your back!" Becky cried, heading toward him to see it closer. The wounds were jagged, long, and very deep. Blood seeped out, streaking down his side.

"Becky, did Slade release you?" Sloan narrowed his eyes.

"No, he didn't." Slade entered the room, answering for Becky, and he was not happy. "Dammit, Becky, I don't have your results back yet. You shouldn't be up walking around."

"Is he going to be okay?" Becky was past caring about herself. The man lying before her with huge gouges in his body from protecting her was who she cared about at the moment. She was absolutely fine.

"He's a vampire," Slade reminded her. "He's fine, but I need to staple some of these closed so they heal right. Some of them are already healing incorrectly."

A frantic nurse entered the room saying, "Dr. Buchanan, the girl in triage four is missing."

"No, she not," Becky responded. She then sat down in a chair next to Sloan's head. "She's right here and not moving." Her eyes pleaded with Sloan.

He had rested his head on his bare muscular arm, his golden eyes staring at her.

"Please don't make me go," she whispered to him.

"Doctor?" the nurse asked. Slade looked toward Sloan, who shook his head.

"She's fine," Slade said, but didn't sound happy about it. "Check on the results of her tests and see if they've come back, please."

The nurse backed out, leaving them alone.

"If you feel dizzy or weak, you need to lie down right away," Slade warned before he started working on Sloan's back.

Becky watched as Slade stapled Sloan's back. She wasn't squeamish—her son had broken bones and bloodied many parts of his body in the past—so the stapling didn't really bother her. She looked back at Sloan, who was staring at her.

"Novocain is the shit, isn't it?" Becky gave him a small smile.

"I wouldn't know," Sloan replied, adjusting his head. "It doesn't work on us."

"Holy crap." Becky cringed, biting her lip as she looked back at Slade stapling the wounds closed without any numbing medication.

It seemed like forever before Slade was done. She did all the grimacing, hissing, and ouching for Sloan.

"Give it about two days and then I'll take the staples out," Slade told him as he walked over to wash his hands.

"Hey, you didn't wear gloves." Becky frowned at Slade.

"We don't get infections and can't give infections," Slade responded, still sounding a little peeved about her escape from triage.

"Must be nice." Becky watched as Slade walked out of the room without commenting. "Guess I made the doctor mad. Story of my life."

"He only has your best interest in mind. And he takes this shit very serious." Sloan pushed up off the table and stood. He turned to grab the shirt Slade had brought him since his was torn all to hell, but stopped when Becky placed her hand gently on his lower back.

"Thank you," she whispered, tears in her voice. "I can't believe you did this for me."

Silently, Sloan turned and stood before her, his gaze tracing a single tear that had escaped her eye.

"I know you're fast and could have gotten away without being touched, but because you were shielding me…." She tilted her head, swallowing hard. "Just thank you."

"You're welcome," he finally said as he reached up and swiped another tear that had escaped.

"Near-death experiences always make me emotional." Becky sniffed, rolling her eyes.

A small smile tipped his full lips as he cupped her chin with the large hand she had admired on many occasions, then slid it to the back of her head. Leaning down, his eyes never left hers. She placed her hand on his arm to help herself rise.

So many times since seeing this man she had imagined this, but that was nothing compared to what she was experiencing, and he hadn't even kissed her yet.

She placed her free hand on his neck, her thumb creasing his strong chin. Finally, his mouth met hers as his hand left the back of her head, moved to her waist, and pulled her against his body. Her feet actually left the floor. She didn't care; she was safe in his embrace.

His tongue dipped in, tasting her, and she happily let him inside. The kiss was demanding and she gave freely. She moaned, not caring. Never had she been kissed so thoroughly. She knew if this man demanded anything from her at that moment, she would have done it. She was in deep shit and she didn't care.

Sloan pulled away, causing a disappointed groan to escape Becky's lips. He set her down on her feet as her gaze met his. His eyes were as black as night. Turning, he put his shirt on right before the door opened. Slade walked in, but Sloan stayed turned away, cracking his neck back and forth.

"Your test results are negative." Slade handed her the release papers. "But next time I put you in a room, if there is a next time, I will tie you down until I release you."

"I'm sorry." Becky signed the paperwork and handed it back to Slade. "I was just freaking out and didn't want to be alone."

Some of the anger left Slade's expression before he headed toward the door. "You're both released," Slade informed them. "I signed yours, boss."

"Thanks," Sloan answered, his voice deep. "Tell the guys I'll be there in a minute."

"Will do." Slade closed the door behind him.

Becky wasn't sure what to do since Slade still had his back to her. It said so much. Finding her voice, Becky attempted an even tone. "Well, I guess I'll see you tomorrow."

When he didn't say anything, her stomach dipped in hurt. She shrugged aside the sensation and headed for the door. A strong arm stopped her and turned her.

"I don't do relationships." Sloan glared down.

Confusion dipped Becky's brows. His anger was palpable, but at what, at who? Wow, she was sounding like Dr. Seuss.

"Ah, okay. Good to know," she replied, not knowing how to reply to that statement. "Though the last time I checked, but then again I've been out of the game for a while, a kiss doesn't constitute a relationship."

Once again Sloan did that silent stare thing. It was actually a real turn-on because a sexy man deep in thought as he stared at her got her imagination flowing.

"Good to know," he finally decided to say. A second later, he pulled her to him and kissed her hard, but she gave as good as she received. Just as abruptly he let her go.

She stumbled back, but he steadied her before going to the door. "I'll have someone take you and Katrina home," Sloan said before disappearing out the door.

Becky stood staring at the closing door, her hand on her mouth. "What the fuck just happened?" she asked the empty room. Unfortunately, the room didn't answer and she left more confused than she'd ever been in her life.

Chapter 21

Sloan had to get the fuck out of that room and fast. Never had his emotions been so involved with a woman, and he had only kissed her, that was it. Nothing else. Just a fucking kiss that blew his mind. Dammit, he needed to hit something.

Seeing his Warriors waiting for him, he went straight to them, ready for any news that could lead him toward the sons of bitches who'd fucked his day up. When he searched their eyes, he knew they were just as ready.

"What did we find out?" Sloan stopped, waiting for the answer.

"Not much," Duncan replied, not looking happy about the fact. "Everything that was in that car was destroyed, and we went through it more than once."

"Did you question the carpenters?" Sloan questioned, his mind still on Becky.

"They said the car was there when they arrived this morning, but they didn't pay much attention to it," Jared answered, his eyes narrowed in anger and frustration.

Sloan felt the same. They had shit to go on. Nothing. "Anyone from the other chapters find anything? Any clue as to who, once again, is after us?"

"Not yet," Duncan replied. "Steve and Adam are camping out at the warehouse to see if anyone shows up to see their handiwork."

"Let's head back there and recheck to see if we missed something." Sloan turned just as Becky headed straight toward him. "I need someone to take Becky and Katrina to Becky's."

Dammit, he was hoping to get the fuck out before he had to face her again. He wasn't a pussy, but he needed to get his head on straight and figure this shit out.

"I can drop them off then meet you guys at the warehouse." Sid stepped in. "I drove the van."

"Okay, good." Sloan turned away, looking for a way out, but passing Becky was the only option. She had that look on her face, one he wasn't used to. When he had sex with women, he'd always leave immediately. No ties, no talk, just in and out, literally. Her look was asking for something more, and he wasn't sure he even knew how to do more.

"Hey." Becky walked up to Sloan, her eyes searching. "I forg—"

"Listen, we are really in a hurry." Sloan barely looked at her. "Sid is going to drive you guys to your place."

"Ah, okay." Becky frowned up at him. "But I—"

"I said we're in a hurry." This time Sloan's tone was rude and dismissive. It was his way, the only way he knew.

"Am I off the clock?" Becky said just as rudely.

"What?" Sloan's head snapped back in confusion.

"Am I off the clock?" she repeated, looking at him like he was an idiot.

"Yes," he replied, not really understanding what she was asking.

"Good! I wasn't coming out here to slobber all over you, and fuck you for thinking I was, asshole," she snapped, poking him in the chest. "The day we came back from the warehouse, there was a dark blue sedan that kept pace with us on the way back to the compound. It slowed at the drive when we pulled in, then took off. It had a dented driver door and dark tinted windows. I didn't think much of it until just a few minutes ago. After the blast today, I saw it again after we hit the ground. Whoever was in that car may have something to do with what happened today, but then again, I'm just a secretary and don't know shit. So take it however you want."

Everyone was silent and looking anywhere but at him, except for Becky who stared at him with no fear, no expectation. No, her stare was filled with distrust and it actually made him, Sloan Murphy, feel like a piece of shit.

"I didn't mea—" Sloan whispered to her as he reached out, but she stepped back.

"Katrina, are you ready?" She turned away from him and, with Katrina at her side, she walked away.

"Ah, guess that's my cue." Sid sidestepped Sloan as he followed the women.

Actually, everyone sidestepped Sloan as they headed out. Duncan passed, tossing him his bike keys. "We had your bike brought over," was all he said as he also walked away.

Alone, Sloan stood in the front of the waiting area. Hearing something, he turned to see an old man who was making his way toward him, his cane clicking on the tile floor.

"Son, that's no way to talk to a pretty lady." He tsked, shaking his head as he passed. "Especially a beauty like that."

Sloan watched as the old man made his way into a room. Running his hand down his face, he cursed. His day had gone to hell, but what surprised him was he'd single-handedly opened hell's door, because just five minutes earlier, he'd been in heaven, he had no doubt.

Shaking his head at those thoughts, he walked through the hallway and happened to look into the room the old man had disappeared into. There he stood, next to the bed, holding the hand of an old woman, his face full of love as he stared down at her still form. Suddenly, the man's face rose toward Sloan. Unshed tears made the old man's eyes bright. Then he dismissed Sloan to look back down at the woman, who was saying something that made the old man smile.

Making his feet move, Sloan continued down the hallway and knew the wise old man was right. He should have never treated Becky that way and he regretted it. She was better off without him. He was not mate material. She would be better off without him. The repeated thought banged around in his brain, making him wonder who he was trying to convince.

******

Becky, with Katrina at her side, followed Sid. No one said a word, but her mind was busy talking and it wouldn't shut up. She was so mad, hurt, and, well, mad. Did Sloan think she was that hard up that she would come running up to him in front of everyone like a lost dog looking for a pat on the head and scraps of his affection? Did he think she was that desperate for him, or any man for that matter?

"Hey, where you going?" Sid called out.

Stopping, Becky realized she'd passed Sid and Katrina. They both stood next to a black van. Silently, she turned, headed back, and climbed into the back of the van. Once Sid and Katrina were buckled up, Sid glanced at her in the rearview mirror before starting the van.

"Where to?" Sid asked before pulling out.

Becky rattled off the address, then leaned back in the seat and closed her eyes, wishing... hell, wishing for what? That she had never met Sloan? That he'd never kissed her? That she found him disgusting like any sane person would find their boss? Seriously, what the hell was wrong with her that she wanted to bang her boss? That wasn't normal, was it?

"You seriously need to block," Sid said from the front seat.

"What?" Becky said absently, then her eyes widened. "What? Are you reading me?"

"Kind of hard not to when your thoughts are so loud." Sid frowned at her in the mirror. "Sloan's an asshole, but a good guy."

Becky shrugged. "Stop reading me or whatever it is you vampires do. It's rude. Or is rude just part of the vampire culture? Because there's a lot of rudeness going on tonight," she rambled. Sighing, she leaned her head back against the seat again, but not before she threw Sid a warning glare.

After a few minutes of silence, the sound of Sid's voice made her open her eyes. "What?"

"Did you say the sedan had a dented driver-side door?" Sid asked, his tone not light and airy, but all business.

"Yes, why?" Becky sat a little straighter, looking into the front where Sid and Katrina sat.

Sid turned the van in the middle of the road but kept his slow speed. "Is that it?"

Becky peered through the windows and then she spotted it. "That's it!" Becky put her face closer to the window to watch the car pass.

Sid was on the phone. "We got the car."

"Where are you going?" Becky watched as they passed the sedan. "That's it. Stop!"

Sid rattled off the address before hanging up. He then parked up the street facing the blue sedan. "Katrina, get in the back."

Katrina quickly relocated and sat next to Becky.

"I'm going to check it out. I want you both to stay put." Sid started to open his door, but turned to look at them. "I mean it. Stay put. If you see anything, text me, but do not get out of this van. No one can see you in here."

"But—" Becky frowned.

"Stay in the van." His growled order cut her off.

Both Becky and Katrina remained in the back of the van unseen, but leaned far enough to watch Sid disappear into the darkness. Scanning the area, Becky realized that a lot of the buildings were vacant. She hoped to hell Sid found whoever owned that car, but she prayed the rest of the Warriors arrived before he did.

"Look." Katrina tugged on her sleeve.

A man stepped out of a building across the street from the car and from where Sid had disappeared. "Dammit," Becky hissed, looking around for Sid. "Text Sid."

"I don't have my phone anymore," Katrina whispered, sounding worried and a little nervous.

Becky pulled out her phone, found Sid's number, hit New Message and typed, MAN HEADING TO CAR, and then, BE CAREFUL! Before she could hit Send, the dreaded sound filled the car. Her phone had died.

"Noooooo!" Becky stared at it as if willing it to come back to life. "Piece-of-shit battery-sucking phone!"

"He's getting in the car," Katrina whispered, once again tugging at her.

Staring out the window, Becky didn't see Sid anywhere. He was probably searching inside the empty buildings on the side of the road the car was parked. Her eyes fell on the keys still in the ignition, then back to the guy. Her eyes went from the man, who was now in the car, to the keys. She couldn't let him get away.

"Put your seat belt on," Becky said as she climbed into the front.

"What are you doing?" Katrina asked, but did as she was told.

Becky turned the key, and the engine purred to life. "Either saving the day or something very stupid." She reached up to the gear shift and put it in drive. "We'll find out in a minute. Hold on."

She inched her way forward, leaving the headlights off. As soon as the car's headlights came on, she knew this was it—now or never. Slamming on the gas, she headed straight for the car's driver-side door.

"Hold on!" Becky screamed before ramming the blue sedan into the telephone pole, blocking the passenger doors. Even knowing she was going to make impact and because she had forgotten to put on her own seat belt, her head banged against the steering wheel. "Are you okay?"

When Katrina didn't answer, she looked in the back to see Katrina staring out the van window. Her gaze followed to see six men rushing toward them with guns drawn.

"I'm thinking we didn't save the day," Katrina finally said, her eyes going to Becky.

Surely Sid had heard the crash, but where in the hell was he? Looking around frantically, she did the only thing that might save their asses. She pressed her hand on the horn.

Both Katrina and Becky screamed when the back window of the van shattered. Holy shit, they were shooting at them. Thoughts of Frankie flashed through her mind and she realized how much of an idiot she had been to take a chance like this. A little adventure was fine, but this had been a huge mistake. She wasn't a Warrior and she definitely wasn't a vampire. She could fucking die. Didn't she just go through this a few hours ago with the explosion?

"Get on the floor." Katrina pushed her down while lowering herself.

"Oh my God." Becky panicked, her brain closing down as bullets ripped into the van. "My son! I can't die. I'm so sorry."

Katrina grabbed her arm, jerking her. "You are not going to die." She then tilted her head toward the top of the van and closed her eyes.

A swooshing noise circled the van, everything became pitch-black, and the shooting stopped. Slowly, Becky lifted her head to peer out the window. Hundreds of bats swarmed the van. She could hear male screams in the distance.

It seemed like forever that the bats flew around the van, protecting them. In the midst of the noise, they heard men shouting their names. Katrina once again closed her eyes and the bats as one flew into the air and disappeared. The driver-side door was pulled off; not opened, but torn off the hinges, and strong arms pulled Becky from her spot under the dashboard.

"Son of a bitch." Sloan's voice sounded worried and on edge. "Are you hit?"

She actually had to think about that one because she honestly didn't know, but she didn't think she was because she didn't hurt anywhere. Or maybe she was just too numb with fear.

Sloan's hands were all over her, turning her as he looked her over. She saw Blaze helping Katrina out of the van and then she saw it, the van. It was riddled with bullet holes, the windows shot out. Her hand went to her mouth as she realized how close she had come to death for a second time.

"Katrina?" Becky whispered toward Katrina, vomit stuck in her throat.

"Is fine." Sloan turned her toward him and searched her face, which was crumpling in the realization of what could have happened. "But are you?"

Becky looked up at him, and everything hit at once. Her hands went to her face as sobs racked her body. She heard Sloan curse, which caused more uncontrollable sobs. She couldn't stop. Her emotions and body were in control and they were a mess. When she was pulled into a hard body, she wrapped her arms around Sloan's neck, climbing up his body until her legs were around his waist. Safe. She prayed as she sobbed that he wouldn't reject her, and he didn't. His strong arms enveloped her and she felt herself being carried away. To where, she didn't care, as long as it was him taking her.

Chapter 22

Sloan carried her a short distance away so he could get her under control, get himself under control. When his team had pulled up and he'd seen the van surrounded by fucking bats—that were also attacking six men with guns—he totally lost it. Sloan never lost it, but he knew that she was in the van and his only thought was getting to her.

When Sid had jumped from the roof and run toward the van, his face a mask of worry and rage, Sloan had laid his bike down and taken off. Becky and Katrina were alone in that van. Damon, Duncan, Jared, Adam, Jill, and Steve all surrounded the men being attacked as he, Sid, and Blaze headed toward the vehicle screaming Becky's and Katrina's names, hoping to be heard above the noise of the bats.

Suddenly, as one, the bats slowed, then rose in the air and disappeared into the night. Once he saw the van riddled with bullet holes, he roared out her name. The first door he went to was the driver side, which he ripped from the van only to see her curled up on the floor under the dashboard. Never in his life had he been more frightened of anything than the thought of losing her; it was a moment in his long life that he would never forget, and for some unknown reason, a flash of memory of the old man standing next to the old woman's bed slammed into him.

Stopping far enough away from the scene, but close enough if he was needed, Sloan continued to hold Becky. Her sobs of terror were just hiccups and sniffs of fear, but her body shook against him.

"You're safe now," he said into her hair, trying to keep any anger out of his voice. "Becky, you're safe." His neck was wet from her tears.

Sid came running up, his expression worried. "Please tell me she's okay?"

"You are a lucky son of a bitch, Sinclair," Sloan growled, rage burning deep inside him. "What in the fuck were you thinking, leaving them alone?"

"No!" Becky pulled her head out of Sloan's neck. "We were safe. He made sure of it. It's my fault, not his."

Sloan made a noise in his throat at her words, but kept quiet. He would deal with Sid later.

"Please, I'm sorry." Becky tried to make it right. "We saw the guy heading toward the car. Katrina didn't have her phone to warn Sid and mine died before I could send the message, so I made a stupid decision to help you."

Sloan agreed silently that it was a stupid decision, one that almost got her killed. She unwrapped her legs from around him and slid to the ground with his help. Wiping her eyes, then her nose, she looked up at Sid, then him.

"I wanted to help and I knew that car had something to do with today, so I rammed the guy until Sid could get there." Becky cleared the tears out of her throat. "I didn't realize there would be more. I was just trying to help so you could find out who was behind the bombing today, so no one else would get hurt. And I didn't want him to get the upper hand on you."

The anger left Sid's face as he ran his hand through his hair. "What you did was brave, Becky," Sid acknowledged, but then frowned. "But fucking stupid. You could have gotten killed, and on my watch. That is something that I can't even imagine. No one, and I mean no one, gets killed on my watch."

"I'm sorry." Becky bowed her head, her lip trembling. "But it wasn't me that was brave. Katrina was the brave one."

Sloan gave Sid a nod. "I'll be there in a minute."

After Sid left, Sloan turned Becky around and lifted her face to his. "Never put yourself in danger like that again," Sloan ordered, but made sure his voice remained calm and even.

Becky nodded as tears filled her eyes again. "I should have never put Katrina in that kind of danger." She reached up and wiped her cheek. "And my son, what if something had happened…?" She couldn't finish as sobs once again wracked her body.

Taking her back in his arms, Sloan held her tight. He'd seen this before—she was in shock and the what-ifs were hitting her hard. It was a normal reaction, especially from someone who was not in the "danger" business.

"I'm not a Warrior. I'm a secretary," she mumbled into his chest. "I would suck as a Warrior and I don't want to die and leave my son with only his asshole father," she babbled between hiccups of tears.

Sloan actually smiled at her words. The Becky he knew was coming around, but he needed to speed it up. He looked over her head to his Warriors, who were pulling the van back to get the fucker out of the sedan. Leaning back, he looked down into her beautiful, wet face.

"Did you get my tux?" Sloan asked after wiping the smile off his face.

"What?" Becky frowned up at him.

"My tux?" Sloan used his thumb to catch another tear. "Did you get it?"

"No, I've been busy getting blown up, ramming cars, and getting shot at," she replied with an angry glare.

"As long as you make sure I have it by Saturday afternoon." Sloan leaned his head close to hers. "And while you're at it, pick up an evening dress for yourself."

"For what?" Becky lifted her shirt, revealing a bit of stomach, to wipe her face.

"I need a date." Sloan took his eyes off her pale skin to look into her eyes. "And as part of your secretary duties, I'm taking you. And yes, that's an order." His lips twitched slightly.

Becky looked back at the mess she'd created and then to Sloan. "After all of that, you're asking me for a date?"

Sloan also looked at the chaos and thought for a minute before nodding. "Yes, I am." His gaze met hers and he was glad her eyes had cleared, but the shaking hadn't stopped. He knew that may take a while. At least she had stopped crying and was no longer thinking of the consequences her actions could have brought her. "These functions are a pain in my ass. I forget names all the time so I need you there to help me keep shit straight."

Swallowing hard, Becky nodded as her eyes welled up again. "You're keeping me?"

If Sloan had a heart, it would have been tugged. Those words alone said so much. "Yes, I'm keeping you," Sloan whispered to her, then winked. "For now," he teased, then chuckled when she smiled.

He led her to the group, his eyes and senses open to any danger. With one arm wrapped protectively around her, ready to pull her to safety, he glanced down and saw her looking at the van.

"Don't worry, I have insurance," he once again teased, trying to keep her mind off what could have happened. But he knew it wouldn't last. Being human and realizing that your life was truly fragile was something one didn't get over quickly.

******

Becky had no idea how she was walking. Her whole body shook and quivered, while her eyes kept returning to the bullet-hole-riddled van. How she and Katrina didn't get shot was a miracle.

She turned to see the six men on their stomachs with Warriors surrounding them. Sloan led her to where Katrina stood with Adam and Steve.

"Don't let her out of your sight," he ordered them before walking away.

Becky watched him walk away, then turned toward Katrina. "Are you okay?"

Katrina nodded, then grinned. "Yes, are you?"

Nodding, Becky didn't know whether to laugh or cry, again. "I'm so sorry."

"It's no big deal. I'm just glad you're okay." Katrina reached out and hugged her. "This is what I'm training for."

"Okay, dammit." Steve stepped in. "For the record, I'm glad you guys are okay, but shit, Katrina, I'm really upset."

"Why?" Katrina frowned.

"Because this is going to be talked about for a long time. Bats? I mean, come on!" Steve threw his hands around. "You fucking commanded bats to come and protect you. What the fuck? Why does everybody get the cool powers and I don't have squat, diddly squat, nada, nothing. It's bullshit!"

"Diddly squat?" Adam gave Steve a sideways glance.

"Yeah, fucking diddly squat," Steve spat out. "I'm sick and tired of waiting for my power when everyone else has one. It's bullshit." Steve kicked a rock and farted.

Adam busted out laughing, as did Katrina and Becky. Becky was the first to stop because she felt so sorry for Steve, but even at a time like this, he made her laugh and it was something she needed so badly.

"Oh, great!" Steve dropped his head back and stared at the sky. "Thanks for having my back!" he shouted toward the heavens.

"You know, Steve." Adam was still laughing and holding his stomach. "That could be your power. Killer farts."

Becky covered her mouth, hiding her grin as Steve actually seemed to consider that. "You know"—Steve frowned then looked pissed—"that probably is my fucking power. I've had a lot of lethal gas lately. Dammit!"

Jared was just walking up as Steve stormed off. "Hey, what's wrong?"

"I fucking farted!" Steve shouted as he marched off.

Becky couldn't help it, she laughed so hard she cried. God love Steve. She needed that so bad. Just when she thought she was going to lose her mind with what had transpired in the last few hours, Steve had found a way to make her forget and laugh.

"What the hell was that all about?" Jared asked, still watching Steve pace around.

"Don't ask," Adam warned, between laughing. "God, that kid is going to kill me one day."

Sloan had also walked up, his eyes following Steve. "What's wrong with Steve?"

"He farted is about all I know." Jared frowned, then looked at Becky, Katrina, and Adam, who were trying to stop laughing.

"Jesus." Sloan shook his head. "What the fuck is wrong with that kid?"

Adam started to talk, but couldn't. He just turned to walk toward Steve, waving whatever he was going to say away. "I can't."

Becky finally stopped laughing. She didn't want to get Steve in trouble. They were in a serious situation; hell, she'd almost died, but one thing she had learned in her short time was the Warriors had a definite sense of humor at the strangest time. Or maybe the right time.

"We are going to take you and Katrina back to the compound." Sloan led her to his bike. "It's closer and we really need to question these assholes."

"We can get a cab," Becky volunteered with a frown. "I don't want to be a bother. I know you have more important stuff here to do."

Sloan slid on his bike and stared at her. "Get on the bike, Becky."

Knowing it would be fighting a losing battle, she hopped on behind him and wrapped her arms around his firm waist. Yeah, she could get used to this. What the hell was she talking about? She was already used to it.

Deciding to not even look toward the van, she rested her head on his back and closed her eyes, trusting Sloan completely.

Chapter 23

Sloan headed toward the interrogation rooms. He had let Becky, who was asleep on her feet, go into his private room to lie down. It took everything he had not to undress her, lay her down, and bury himself deep inside her. Tonight had opened his eyes to his exact feelings for Becky Spencer and it went beyond fucking her.

Hitting the elevator button, he cursed as the doors shut and he leaned against the wall. This was it. He knew it. He felt it. She was his fucking mate and he felt sorry for her. He was demanding, a prick, and had no time for anyone other than his duties. She would end up hating him, but he seriously didn't know if he could live without her.

Slamming the Stop button on the elevator, Sloan slid down the wall into a crouched position, his head in his hands as he tried to clear his thoughts. He'd known that if he'd found her dead inside that van he would have taken his own life. Only a mated male would have thought that way and meant it. She was doomed by his hand.

"Goddammit!" Sloan stood and punched the elevator wall, denting the steel. It was not supposed to happen to him. He wasn't supposed to find his mate. He had made it his main priority to steer clear of any feelings toward a woman. Regardless, she'd appeared in his life and before he knew what was happening… that was a lie. He'd known it, felt it the first time he'd laid eyes on her, yet he hadn't fought hard enough to let her go. He was a selfish bastard. He wanted her. Plain and simple.

She was his and no other motherfucker would ever have her. "Shit!" Sloan cursed at his thoughts, panic throbbing through him. And wouldn't the other Warriors get a fucking kick out of this shit. Not that he really cared. He could take their shit, but he didn't want to hear it. He was having a hard enough time accepting it himself.

Knowing he needed to get to work, he hit the button again and the elevator began to move. The doors opened and he stomped down the hall, busting into one of the rooms.

"Anything?" he growled at Duncan, who watched Jared and Sid interrogate one of the six men who had shot up the van.

"Oh, yeah. They're telling everything." Duncan nodded with an angry frown. "And it's not good. It looked like anti-vampire humans are taking things into their own hands. Seems they feel if they get rid of the VC Warriors, then the human government will have to take over and kill all the vampires because there will be no vampire justice with us gone."

"You have got to be kidding me." Sloan leaned closer to get a look at the asshole in the chair; he looked scared to death. Understandable, since Jared and Sid looked pretty intimidating.

"Wish I was," Duncan replied. "Seems it's just random acts, no set plan. Total chaos. They even have a Facebook page for them to boast about how many Warriors or trainees they kill."

Sloan looked at the laptop Duncan scooted toward him. Disgusted, Sloan scrolled through the page before slamming it shut. "You informed the other chapters?"

"I'm streaming the interrogation to them now," Duncan replied, hitting a few buttons. "They are seeing it live, just as we are."

"What about the guy in the sedan?" Sloan stared into the interrogation room.

"He's a scout. They drive around finding the locations and putting them on the page. Whoever wants it, takes it." Duncan opened the laptop and searched before shoving the computer back toward Sloan. "They also take pictures to post."

Sloan looked down and his eyes changed instantly to black as rage filled him. Staring at him was Becky, her eyes wide with fear as he lay on top of her, protecting her right after the blast.

"Over 5,000 people have liked their page and seen that photo."

Duncan nodded toward the computer. "This isn't good. There is no organization and so far, we haven't found a name of a leader. If this truly is an unorganized group, we are fucked."

Once again, Sloan's eyes fell on Becky's picture and the fear in her eyes was his undoing. Slamming out of the room, he headed straight for the interrogation room, almost ripping the door off its hinges. Walking past Sid and Jared, who got out of his way, Sloan picked the human up by the throat and slammed him against the wall.

"You have five fucking seconds to give me a name, motherfucker." Sloan's face and fangs were inches from the terrified man's face. "Before I rip your goddamn throat out."

The man sputtered something, but was too terrified to speak legible English. Sloan slammed him against the wall once again and tightened his grip.

"Time's up!" Sloan opened his mouth and tilted his head, an inhuman growl leaving his throat. The man screamed.

"Okay!" he managed to get past his closed-off throat.

"Okay, what, you piece of shit?" Sloan straightened out his arm so the man went higher on the wall.

"Evan Nico is the name I've heard," the man squeaked out. "That's all I know. I swear it."

Sloan glared at the man for a few more minutes. "Get Adam in here, now."

"He's interrogating with Blaze in another room. Hold on." Sid rushed out and then came right back with Adam.

"Evan Nico?" Sloan questioned.

"Seems that name is popping up with all of them." Adam nodded, then looked at the ground where Sloan had dropped the man. He lay on the floor, crying.

Sloan looked toward the two-way mirror. "Run that name," Sloan ordered, then turned to leave the room. "I want that son of a bitch and I want him now."

"What do you want us to do with these guys?" Jared asked, grinning at the man on the floor.

"Lock them up." Sloan didn't even glance at the sobbing man.

"Should we give him some clean clothes?" Jared raised his eyebrows then creased his nose. "I think he shit himself."

"Damn, Sloan." Sid backed out of the room, waving his hand in front of his face. "You literally scared the shit out of him. I'm fucking impressed."

Sloan didn't answer as he disappeared down the hallway. He was pissed beyond words. To see Becky's terrified face on a page where others could enjoy her fear was a huge mistake for those fuckers. Evan Nico, whoever the fuck he was, had signed his own death warrant.

******

Waking with a jolt, Becky shot up in bed. She looked around frantically, the events of the blast all coming back to her. She was in Sloan's private room at the compound. With a calming sigh, she grabbed her phone off the small table and squinted at the time. Eight in the morning. Her internal clock was a little off, but then again, she'd only fallen asleep a few hours earlier. She tilted her head and strained to hear, but only silence greeted her. Sloan's usually bustling office was silent.

Glancing around, she spotted what appeared to be the bathroom and got up. After doing her business, she glanced at the shower. She felt gross. Even though she didn't have any clean clothes, she figured her body would at least be clean. Picking up a towel on the floor, she sniffed. It smelled like Sloan. She took another long whiff, heat filling her cheeks, forcing her to drop the towel.

Quickly shedding her clothes, she turned the shower on and stepped inside. The water felt amazing. She stood there for a while, letting it pour down her body, over her face, moaning in relief the whole time. Grabbing the soap, she quickly lathered up and then searched for the shampoo. Seeing it near the drain, she bent, poured some in her hand, then scrubbed her hair. Once clean, she relaxed and didn't move until the water started to cool. With a sigh, she turned it off as chill bumps pimpled across her skin.

Peeking out of the shower curtain for the towel, her eyes landed on a pair of boots before her gaze lifted to muscled jeans-covered legs, a nice bulging area, on to a black T-shirt and then finally to Sloan's gorgeous face.

"Looking for this?" He held out the towel on his finger.

"Thought I'd take a quick shower," Becky said, stating the obvious. "Hope that's okay."

His eyes dropped, lingering on her body, then rose again. "You can use my shower anytime."

Becky nodded, glancing down herself to see that the shower curtain was practically see-through. Her eyes shot back up to his. "How long have you been standing there?"

"Long enough." His grin was so masculine it made all her girl parts scream out in need.

"Well, that wasn't very gentlemanly." Becky raised an eyebrow at him, then reached for the towel.

"Never have I admitted to being a gentleman." He cocked his eyebrow right back at her and pulled the towel back toward him so when she reached, she almost took a step out of the shower. "Unfortunately, there are some women out there ready to take you shopping for a dress."

"You were serious about that?" Becky frowned.

"Yes."

"I just thought you were trying to make me feel better." Becky was starting to freeze and was ready for that towel, but he didn't seem to be willing to give it up yet.

"No."

Okay, his one-word responses were about to drive her crazy. No, that was a lie. It was his stare; he had such an intense stare. A stare so bold she wanted to know what he was thinking. She couldn't help but wonder if his thoughts were dirty ones about her.

"Can I have my towel?" Becky knew her voice quivered and it wasn't from being cold.

"Come and get it," he teased with a cocky grin. She could tell by his face he didn't think she would.

One thing about her was she wasn't really shy. She smirked at his challenge. If a man didn't like her body, he could go kick rocks and it would be his loss. Though in all honesty, she would probably die if Sloan looked at her in disgust, but she'd live and then go work out. She chuckled to herself at that thought.

So he had thrown out a dare and she was never one to turn down a dare. Ripping open the shower curtain, Becky stepped out of the shower. She had to give him credit, he showed no emotion other than a flare in his darkening golden eyes.

She held out her hand for the towel. With a growl, he handed it to her as his eyes roamed her body. "Thank you," she said with a prissy tone as she passed him, only putting the towel to her front, her ass bare for his gaze. *Take that, Mr. Warrior.* She grinned, but then gasped when she was pulled up against his hard body.

"You are very lucky that there are people in the other room," he whispered in her ear. One hand wrapped around her waist and the other cupped her breast, squeezing before his hand stroked down her stomach to the V of her thighs, his finger slowly rubbing her entrance.

She leaned her head back against him, moaning softly at his touch. "And why is that?"

"I would be so deep inside you, but I don't believe in twenty-minute fucks." His gravelly voice vibrated against her neck. He bit her softly as his finger penetrated her and then he pulled away and headed for the door.

Becky wanted to shout, "I do! I believe in twenty-minute fucks," but words were beyond her. Her body was on fire, her legs barely keeping her upright, and when he turned to give her a sexy wink, she sighed. She fucking sighed. No man in her life had made her sigh.

"I will pick you up at six tomorrow night," Sloan instructed, all business and bosslike. "You have the rest of the day off. Have a nice day." His smile was the sexiest she'd ever seen. He then walked out and closed the door.

"Ah, but, ah…." She trailed off. Holy shit, she had lost the upper hand, and quickly.

Chapter 24

Becky had tried on so many dresses she was ready to drop in exhaustion. She stood in the dressing room staring at herself, turning this way and that. Being a redhead, it was hard to find colors that didn't clash with her hair. The deep purple she currently wore was the best by far she had tried on. It cut low, but not too low, in the front, making it look classy, not trashy. The dress fit her form, and her ass didn't look huge. She looked in proportion and that wasn't easy with her body type. With a sigh, she stepped out of the room to face the fashion police waiting for her.

"Okay." She spread her arms wide. "Please tell me this is the one because I honestly don't know if I can try on another."

"Wow!" Caroline stood, then turned her around, and stepped back. "That is amazing and the color is stunning on you."

"Absolutely, the one." Nicole grinned as Tessa nodded in agreement.

"Thank God!" Becky went to sink into a chair, but stopped when they yelled.

"Don't wrinkle it!"

Becky sighed, glancing at the chair longingly. She had finally met most of the mates. Nicole, Tessa, Pam, Lana, Angelina, and Caroline were amazing women. Katrina and Jill weren't able to come because of training.

"Well, let me get this off so I can collapse." She turned to head to the dressing room, but heard her phone. Reaching over, she picked up and grinned. "It's my son, Frankie."

Answering, she held the phone out. He was Facetiming her. "It is so good to see your handsome face." She smiled and felt tears, but held them back.

"Hey, Mom!" Frankie smiled, then frowned. "What are you wearing?"

Laughing, she moved the phone so she could show him her dress. "I have a function I'm going to with my new boss." She brought the phone back up. "What do you think about that?"

"Dude, your mom is hot!" another voice came over the phone.

"Shut up, Mike." Frankie punched out and there was a loud commotion over the phone before Frankie came back into view. "Sorry, Mom."

"Is that your roommate?" Becky chuckled.

"Yes." Frankie rolled his eyes, but grinned.

"Hi, Ms. Spencer!" A face popped up behind Frankie.

"Hello, Mike." Becky narrowed her eyes. "You boys behaving?"

"Totally," they answered in unison.

"So how's the new job?" Frankie had stood and was walking, making the picture jerky.

"It's good. And everyone is so nice." Becky drank her son's face in. God, how she missed him.

"I still can't believe you're working for a vampire, a VC Warrior, *the* VC Warrior." Frankie did sound awed by the fact. "Those guys are badass."

If he only knew, Becky thought, but didn't say anything. "Hey, I have some new friends I'd like you to meet. They're mates to some of the warriors."

"Cool." Frankie smiled and Becky wondered how many girls were chasing her little boy because he was so handsome. Okay, Momma Bear needed to chill out.

Turning her phone, she aimed it toward the women. "This is Nicole, Tessa, Angelina, Pam, Lana, and Caroline."

"Hi, Frankie!" they all said and waved.

"Don't worry. Your mom is being well taken care of." Caroline smiled into the phone.

"Hi!" Frankie smiled with Mike in the background.

"Damn, we need to go visit your mom," Mike said.

"Will you shut up?" Frankie sounded irritated. "Hey, thanks. I hate her being there alone."

"Well, we got her." Nicole called out. "No worries!"

"It was nice meeting you!" They all waved as Becky turned the phone back toward her.

"I miss you," she said into the phone. "Are you eating enough? Are you okay on money?"

"I miss you too, Mom, and yes, I'm fine. Stop worrying." Frankie chuckled.

"I'm your mom. It's my job to worry." Becky grinned then sniffed, not wanting to cry, but dammit, it was hard.

"So is your boss nice?" Frankie abruptly changed the subject.

Her cheeks heated. "Yes, he's nice as far as bosses go."

"Mom?" Frankie tilted his head, staring at her. "Are you blushing? Are you crushing on your boss?"

"Stop changing the subject, Frankie," she scolded, glancing at the women, who grinned at her. "How're your grades?"

Frankie laughed. "They're fine, Mom." They were both silently staring at each other. "I'm glad you got friends. It's time you enjoy your life. I'm fine."

Okay, that got her. Dammit. She sniffed, her son's face blurring. "You take care of yourself."

"And you have fun on your… date." He grinned.

"It's not a date. It's a function." Becky rolled her eyes then wiped a tear away.

"Whatever," he teased. "Love you, Mom. I'll call you sometime this weekend."

"Love you, too." She waited until he disappeared before she let her tears flow.

The women surrounded her, offering comfort where they could. "You have a one-in-a-million son, Becky." Nicole gave her a nod. "And he loves his momma very much."

"He is the best." Becky sniffed through her tears. "I just miss him so damn much."

Tessa wiped her eyes, then smiled. "I think this calls for lunch and ice cream."

"Hell yeah, it does." Lana turned Becky around, leading her to the dressing room. "Let's get this dress and a pair of shoes, then go eat and have some girl talk."

"Since when do you do girl talk?" Caroline glanced at her sister with a surprised grin.

"Hey, I'm learning," Lana replied, pushing Becky inside the room and shutting the door.

Becky held her phone to her chest, wanting so badly to call Frankie back, but she wouldn't. She had to keep reminding himself he was no longer a young boy, and she had to ease herself out of his life so he could live his. Damn, no one said being a mom would hurt so damn much.

******

When Sloan's gaze landed on the burnt spot in the warehouse parking lot, rage beat through his body. The car was gone, but the evidence of the explosion remained.

Walking inside, his eyes focused on the trainees working on mitts. His eyes fell on Ben, who was pretty damn good, but his attitude sucked, which was a damn shame. His eyes fell on Katrina. She was fast, but her hits were light, as if not wanting to hurt the person holding the pads.

"You ready for them?" Jax asked, stepping toward him. When Sloan nodded, Jax turned around. "Everyone stop, come this way, and take a knee."

Sloan waited, watching each of them. Not a one of them made eye contact with him, other than Katrina, but she looked away quickly.

"I guess by now you have all heard what happened here and at other training facilities across the city." Sloan waited for them to answer before continuing. "I want everyone on alert. We are not going to stop training. I have set up cameras on the property here. Each one of you will take shifts to be on watch. One person steps foot on this property, I want to know about it ASAP. If you fail at your shift, you will not enjoy the consequences."

"Yes, sir."

One brave soul actually raised his hand. "When does this start and how do we know when our shift is?"

"We already have one of you monitoring now," Blaze replied as the group looked around to see who was missing. "The system is set up at the compound. The list of shifts and times are posted on the back wall. If you have a problem with your time, tough shit. Be there. If you fail to show, you are out of the program."

"Yes, sir."

"Any questions?" Sloan asked, once again staring them down. "Good. Now get your asses busy."

Jax stayed behind while Blaze took over. "Any new news?" Jax asked, his eyes focused on the trainees.

"No, but I'm hoping some information will come tomorrow night," Sloan replied, also watching the trainees. "I have that fucking function bullshit again and Mayor Groper will be there as well as a few other council members. Hopefully spreading the word about these assholes may give us some information."

"True." Jax grinned, then tried to hide it with his hand.

"What?" Sloan had seen him from the corner of his eye and frowned.

"Nothing." Jax cleared his throat.

"What are they betting and how much is at stake?" Sloan cursed. Dammit, he'd known it was coming.

"That she'll come in to work tomorrow all rosy and satisfied." Jax chuckled, then stepped away from Sloan when he growled. "And it's pretty up there."

"What in the hell is wrong with you guys?" Sloan hissed with a shake of his head. "Fucking assholes."

"Hey, you do these functions all the damn time and this is the first time you've taken a woman." Jax held up his hands. "You were just asking for this, my friend."

"Yeah, well, fuck you and fuck Jared and Sid, who I know are behind the betting." Sloan turned to leave, still muttering. "This shit is going to stop. No more betting. I'm the boss and what I say goes."

"Hey, I've seen you take a few bets in my time here," Jax reminded him.

"It wasn't about me, so that was fine," Sloan said and meant it. "This shit will stop."

"Have fun tomorrow night." Jax chuckled, hurrying onto the mat.

"Fuck you, Jax." Sloan walked out the door with a sigh. Fucking assholes!

Chapter 25

Becky stared at herself in the mirror, hoping she looked okay. After lunch with the girls, she had gone home and passed out until early that morning. She had kept herself busy cleaning and running errands. But it being time to leave, she was a nervous damn wreck.

She had actually cleaned with her new heels on just to make sure she wouldn't make a fool out of herself. She would die if she embarrassed not only herself, but Sloan.

She didn't even know what kind of function they were actually going to, other than it required a tux and evening gown. It was a first for her, and looking into her terrified expression, it showed.

The knock on her door made her jump. Her breathing became erratic. Taking a deep breath, she locked eyes on herself in the mirror. "You can do this!"

Before her reflection could say otherwise, she walked out of the bathroom to the front door. Opening it, she gasped and actually wobbled on her heels. Sloan stood staring down at her, his eyes roaming her body as his eyes darkened.

"Why do your eyes do that?" she asked without thought. She was struck stupid by how damn handsome he looked in a tux. Jeans and T-shirts fit Sloan fine, but a tux was just... holy-shit fine!

A smile curved his lips. "Because I like what I see." He stepped into her house. "You are absolutely beautiful, Becky."

She knew she blushed, but didn't care. "Thank you." Her eyes did some roaming of their own. "And you, well, I'm speechless and that says a lot. I'm never ever speechless."

Sloan leaned his head back an d laughed. "I'll take that as a compliment."

"Definitely a compliment." She smiled up at him, loving his laugh. He should do it more often. Suddenly, she had the urge to make laugh as much as possible—as part of her job as his secretary, of course.

"You ready to do this thing?" He reached for her.

She collected her bag and nodded, letting him lead her out the door. He closed it and made sure it was locked before taking her elbow and escorting her down the steps. "A limo?" she asked, impressed.

"Usually I ride my cycle, but I didn't think that would work very well for tonight." He glanced down at her dress, that hungry, dark look in his eyes.

"Oh, I don't know." Becky grinned. "I think we could have made it work."

"Well, maybe after we leave, we'll take a spin because I'm all kinds of curious now." Sloan's deep voice vibrated around her.

An older man stood next to the open limo door. "Thanks, Hank." Sloan nodded as he helped Becky step into the limo.

"Yes, thank you." Becky smiled at the man before disappearing inside.

"I've never ridden in a limo before." Becky looked around in awe. "It's huge in here."

"Yeah, not real impressed." Sloan frowned, then hit a button and the sunroof opened. "I prefer riding free."

Becky smiled in understanding. Yes, Sloan was not the type to be contained. Sitting close, their legs touched. A happy thrum pulsed through her body at the contact. She glanced to see she had plenty of room and wondered if she should scoot over to give him more space. Ah, hell with it. She stayed right where she was. It was a once in a lifetime moment and she was going to take advantage of everything it had to offer, even sitting leg to leg with the most handsome man she'd ever met.

"You know, I don't think I even asked what this function is. I just knew you needed a tux and like a good secretary"—she smiled sweetly at him—"that's what I did with no questions."

"It's part of the job I despise." Sloan frowned. "Bunch of people who think they are important get together to slap each other on the back."

"Then why do you go?" Becky turned so she could see him better. He really did sound unhappy about going. "We can always skip out."

"Oh, believe me, I think about doing that all the time, but in my position, I don't have the luxury of skipping out. If I can benefit the council in any way by being there, then I'm there," Sloan replied, his voice even and businesslike. "It's like any job, parts of it suck. Honestly, I wouldn't have even remembered this one if the mayor hadn't called me to make sure I was going to be there. I have the invite, but never even looked at it."

Becky laughed, shaking her head. "How about you let me handle your mail so the mayor doesn't have to remind you? That's my job now."

"You most certainly can have it." Sloan's eyebrow rose. "I probably have a stack you can go through Monday."

Nodding, Becky leaned back and looked out the window, not even knowing where they were going.

"Can I ask you a personal question?" Sloan's voice broke the silence.

Okay, that surprised her. What on earth could Sloan want to know personally about her? "Sure." She looked up at him.

"What happened with your marriage?" Sloan's gaze didn't waver.

"Oh, Lord." Becky laughed. "What didn't happen to my marriage?

Let's see, I was a naïve girl at sixteen who had unprotected sex with her first serious boyfriend and got herself pregnant. Frank stayed around for a while, but soon he was gone, only to show up later on down the road."

"He left you to take care of your son, alone?" He frowned, his eyes narrowing.

"But he came back." She tilted her head with a bitter grin. "And dumb me let him. After a few years we got married. I guess I felt having someone, even someone I didn't love, to help me raise a good but rambunctious boy was better than nothing. I settled and I will regret that till the day I die. He broke Frankie's heart more than he helped me. So I took what help I could get from him and once I found him in bed with my best friend, I finally left and filed for divorce."

"I'm sorry," Sloan replied. His tone indicated he really meant it.

"For what? Me being a dumbass?" Becky chuckled and shook her head. She was over that whole period of her life, so she could finally joke about it without breaking down or crying at her own stupidity.

"No." He took her hand in his. "That he wasn't man enough for you or your son."

And wow! She had to look away from the intensity of that statement and his stare. "My only regret is that my son got hurt when all I was trying to do was make it right for him." She sighed, long and loud. "But my son is on the right track and is strong, thank God. None of that seems to have had a lasting effect on him."

"Because of you." Sloan squeezed her hand. "I'd like to meet him someday. He sounds like a good kid."

"Thank you. I did my best with him." Becky hoped she didn't get all teary-eyed and ruin her makeup. Lord, she was as weepy as hell lately and that had to stop. She wasn't an overly emotional woman, except where her son was concerned. "And he is a great kid. I'm sure he'll be showing up to check out where I work sometime soon."

The limo had stopped and there was a tap on the window. Sloan knocked back and the door opened. Sloan stepped out, his hand appearing to help her emerge. She tried to do that as gracefully as possible. Not easy sliding across a leather seat in an evening gown.

Thanking Sloan and the concierge, she glanced up and gasped. "Oh, my God." She stared at the mansion, alight with twinkling lights. "I have a strong feeling I'm not going to fit in here."

Sloan chuckled as he held out his arm for her to slip hers through. "That makes two of us."

"Okay, I'm going to apologize now if I embarrass you," Becky whispered as they made their way to the door. "I will do my best not to."

He stopped in the middle of the sidewalk and stared down at her. She knew people were coming up behind them, but he didn't seem to care.

"You have more class and integrity than anyone inside those walls." He wasn't exactly whispering and again, he didn't seem to care. "Don't let anyone make you feel beneath them or I'll have to…."

"You'll have to what?" She stared up at him, waiting on pins and needles for him to finish.

This time he leaned down, his lips close to her ear. Chills and urges ramped through her body at the closeness of his lips to her skin. "Kill them."

A loud laugh escaped her lips and she slapped her hand over her mouth. "Stop it," she said as they continued toward the party.

******

Sloan could listen to her laugh all day. She had a contagious laugh; even a woman who had passed them looked back and smiled at her. He felt a sense of pride having her on his arm.

Once inside he'd become alert. It was just part of his job, his makeup. Crowds made him edgy. Anything could happen and it wasn't just him he had to think of; she was here with him and his responsibility.

A waiter came by, offering them a glass of wine, but he declined for himself. Becky however, looked up at him for permission and he grinned with a nod.

"I'll just have one." Becky took a sip and moaned. "Since I'm working, but, man, this stuff beats Busch beer."

"You're not on the clock so enjoy yourself." He chuckled, glancing around, then back down at her. "And anything tastes better than Busch beer."

She gave a tilted nod in agreement. "That is true, but it's cheap." She took another drink. "But this stuff isn't."

"Sloan." A man walked toward him, his hand outstretched.

"Hey, George." Sloan shook his hand, noticing how the mayor's eyes kept dropping to Becky. Actually, a lot of males' eyes were dropping to Becky and he wasn't really sure he liked that very much. No, in truth, it was pissing him off. "This is Becky Spencer. Becky, this is Mayor Groper."

"It's nice to meet you." Becky took the mayor's hand.

"Likewise." The major's eyes went to her breasts, which looked fucking amazing in that dress. Sloan really wanted to fucking smash the mayor's face in, and he liked the guy. "George. George!" Sloan finally got his attention.

"Huh, oh. Come. I want you to meet our new DA." George turned to look over the crowd.

"New DA?" Warning signals started going off inside his head and when he had this sensation, he usually wasn't wrong. Something was off. "What happened to Lance, our existing district attorney?"

George stopped and looked at Sloan in surprise. "You didn't hear?"

"Obviously not." Sloan was not happy about this. Why hadn't he been informed they were getting a new district attorney, and what the fuck happened to Lance Garfield?

"He was arrested on heroin charges, among other things," George whispered, then frowned at Sloan. "I can't believe you didn't know about this."

"Been a little busy hunting bad guys and keeping my trainees alive." Sloan was not happy and he knew those around him felt it. He didn't hide his feelings from anyone if he wanted them to know he was pissed, and he wanted their mayor to know he was not happy in the least. There was no way in hell, though, that Lance Garfield was on heroin. Someone had planted the shit; he'd bet his life on it.

"I heard about that." George looked concerned. "Was anyone hurt?"

"No." Sloan's reply was gruff.

"Good, that's good." George once again looked around.

"Are you okay?" Becky tugged on his arm, leaning close.

He nodded, but didn't give her a reassuring smile he usually would. His senses were alert and he knew someone in the fucking room was keeping close tabs on him. He hadn't stayed alive for so long without knowing and trusting his instincts.

"There he is. Stay here." George disappeared. Then just as quickly, he reappeared with a man in tow. "This is Sloan Murphy."

Sloan nodded at the man, trying to get a read on him. He took the hand that was offered and shook. The man had a good grip and was actually trying to prove something with the tight squeeze. It was the man's eyes Sloan didn't trust. He took stock of the man, and his eyes were shifty to say the least. Sloan didn't like him. His assessment was as instinctive as he was sure it was right. Every fucking time.

"This is our new district attorney, Evan Nico." The mayor finished the introductions, not realizing he had just introduced two men who had never met, but were definitely enemies.

A not so subtle smile of "gotcha ya" hit Sloan's lips as a "give it your best shot" grin lit Evan Nico's.

Chapter 26

Katrina sat in the kitchen waiting for someone to give her a ride to Becky's. She was bummed that she hadn't gotten to see Becky before she'd left with Sloan, but training called. Things were going a little better. The guys were mostly leaving her alone, except Ben glared at her constantly, but that she could ignore easily.

Hearing someone come in, she turned to see Steve. "Hey!" She smiled, happy to see him. Steve was awesome, but lately he seemed sad, and that wasn't like him. She hadn't known him long, but he was always cheerful, making jokes.

"What are you doing?" he asked, grabbing something to drink out of the fridge. He then sat down across from her.

"Just waiting for someone to get free to take me to Becky's. She was off today," Katrina replied, wanting to help Steve somehow. He had always been there for her and she felt like she was letting him down.

"I can take you in a little while. I have to hang here until Jax gets back, just in case one of the trainees sees something on the monitor." Steve rolled his eyes. "Fun shit." He took a drink, then stared at the can of soda.

"You'll get your powers, Steve." Katrina leaned over the table and touched his hand.

"I'm seriously doubting it," Steve replied with a sigh. "Hell, I'd even take the toxic farting gig, but that stopped. Go figure, huh."

Katrina chuckled, then felt relief when Steve laughed with her. "Sometimes when we want something so bad it takes forever for it to happen. Just like in school when you wanted the day to end and stared at the clock, it ended up being the longest day ever."

"Yeah, been there done that." Steve leaned back in his chair. "I've always had this problem of wanting something and wanting it now.

I'm not very patient. It's just...."

"Just what?" Katrina urged him.

"I don't want it to be a joke, like toxic farts or something like that." Steve was dead serious. "I know I'm a goof-off, but I take my duties seriously and I want a serious power. Something that will help the Warriors."

"You never know, you may already have the power you're supposed to have, but haven't realized yet." Katrina added, "That's what happened to me."

"Yeah, maybe." Steve flicked the can with his finger. "Sometimes I just want to disappear. Do you ever feel that way?"

"All the time." Katrina nodded. "Usually I do because not a lot of people notice me, which is fine with me. I'm invisible to most anyway."

"What I wouldn't give to be invisible sometimes." Steve shrugged, then sighed. "Yeah, sometimes I wish I was invisible."

Katrina gasped, her chair sliding back and hitting the wall behind her. "Oh my God! Steve!"

"What?" Steve sounded alarmed. "What is it?"

"You're invisible?" Katrina said, shocked, then laughed, her hand on her cheek in disbelief.

"Oh, ha-ha, Katrina." Steve's voice dipped in sadness. "I didn't take you for a cruel person."

"No, I'm totally serious." Katrina stood to get something that showed a reflection. Yanking the chrome toaster off the counter, she all but pulled her arm off when she forgot to unplug it. "Shit!" She hurried and unplugged it, heading toward Steve.

She could see a shimmer of him, but it was truly strange.

"What the hell are you doing with the toaster?" Steve asked, his tone pissy.

"Here! Look!" She held the toaster out, which quickly left her hands. She watched the toaster jerk back and forth, up and down, sideways and upside down. It was a very weird experience watching the toaster float in the air until it dropped on the table. "Steve?"

Suddenly there was a big whoop that filled the room, the chair he had been sitting on was knocked over, and she was picked up off her feet. She was hugged and spun in circles.

"What in the fuck!?" Jared boomed as he walked in.

Katrina was getting dizzy, but she saw Jared and Sid, who had followed him in, staring at her in horror.

"She's possessed." Sid's voice was serious and it kind of scared her.

"Put me down, Steve," Katrina said and she was immediately put on her feet.

"Steve?" Sid walked toward her, looking at her closely. "Katrina, are you okay?"

"I'm fine," Katrina responded, and before she could say anything else, Sid was blocking at something.

"What the fuck?" Sid was in a fighting stance, looking around. "Something just touched me."

Katrina was about to tell Steve to stop when she saw Jared's hair lifting from his shoulder. A giggle slipped past her lips at the look on

Jared's face. His arm shot out and she heard Steve curse.

"Hey, damn," Steve's voice called out. "It's just me."

"No! That's a fuck no!" Jared hissed, a look of disbelief on his face. "This cannot be your fucking power. No!"

"Oh, but it is." Steve laughed gleefully. "Can you believe it? All this time I probably had my power, but didn't know it."

"Jesus!" Sid shook his head. "Okay, enough. Time for us to see you, Steve."

They waited and nothing.

"Am I back?" Steve asked, but they all shook their heads. "Okay, now?"

"No." Jared frowned. "Come on, stop screwing around."

"I'm not." Steve's voice pitched high in panic. "Oh, God. What if I'm stuck like this? I'll never get laid."

Katrina rolled her eyes, walking toward him. Blaze had walked in and was looking at them all like they were crazy. "You wished to be invisible, so just wish to be visible."

Suddenly, Steve shimmered back, his eyes wide with fright. "Am I back?"

"No," Sid said, making Katrina frown.

Steve slapped his hands over his face. "Oh, God. What have I done?" He sank to his knees, his face still in his hands before he looked up to glare at Katrina. "This is all your fault, Katrina."

"You're back, Steve." Katrina sighed, nodding toward Sid. "He was lying."

"I'm back?" Steve leaped up and grabbed the toaster. "Oh, thank God." He then kissed his reflection; actually, he kissed the toaster.

His eyes widened. "I wish for a million dollars!" he shouted, then looked around. So did everyone else. He then looked under the table.

"Ah, I don't think that's how it works." Katrina shook her head. "Your words have nothing to do with it. Your power is invisibility. You just have to use your mind to achieve it. Try it again."

Steve nodded, then frowned. "I'm scared." He glanced at Katrina. "What if I stay that way?"

"You won't." She chuckled, then stopped when her gaze met Blaze's.

Steve once again disappeared, but then reappeared quickly. "Am I here?"

"Yes." Katrina nodded.

"Sweet! I'm going to fuck with Adam and Jill. This is awesome." Steve headed for the door, but stopped and headed toward Katrina to give her the biggest hug. "Thank you!"

Not liking the questioning looks she received from Jared, Sid, and Blaze, she wished she had Steve's power. Since she didn't, she slowly made her way back to the table and sat down.

"Someone is going to kill him," Jared said as he headed further into the kitchen.

"My bet's on Damon," Sid called out, rattling pots and pans. "No, probably going to be Sloan."

"Honestly, do you know how much intel we can get using his power?"

Jared stopped and looked at Sid. "This is pretty huge."

"Guess we need to keep the kid alive then," Sid replied as he continued to prepare for dinner.

Katrina sat listening to them and was amazed by the Warriors. There never was a dull moment. She used her peripheral vision to watch Blaze, who stood staring at her.

"Do you need a ride?" Blaze's voice had her turning toward him.

"If you got time," Katrina replied, hating to be a pain the ass.

"Come on." He held the door open for her.

Katrina called out a good-bye to Sid and Jared as she passed Blaze, careful not to touch him. Yeah, Steve was lucky.

Chapter 27

Becky didn't know exactly what was going on, but something was definitely not right. She felt Sloan's tension as if it were her own. She watched the man he had been introduced to, Evan Nico. He was a big man, but nothing compared to Sloan. His hair was dark and he had a dark exotic look about him. As she studied him, knowing he was the reason for Sloan's different mood, the man looked down at her.

"And who is this lovely lady?" He reached for her hand.

"Becky Spencer." She smiled, but as soon as he touched her hand, she wanted to pull it back. "Nice to meet you," she lied. She could have gone the rest of her life without meeting the man before her. His eyes kept going to her cleavage. The mayor's had also, but the look Evan gave her was different and made her feel dirty.

Finally, Evan looked away, maybe because Sloan casually stepped in front of her, blocking his view.

"Ah, a jealous man, I see." Evan smiled with a nod. "And totally understandable with such a beautiful woman. I've heard a lot of things about you, Sloan Murphy."

"Good," Sloan replied, his voice even, emotionless. Becky noticed that the mayor looked a little nervous, so it wasn't just her feeling the tension. "I'm sure I'll be hearing a lot about you also."

"Oh, of that I have no doubt," the man said, the lightness of his voice darkening. "Heard you've had a little trouble lately."

"Nothing we can't handle," Sloan replied, his shoulders stiff, poised as if ready for something.

"Well, you let me know." Evan took a step. "If you catch any involved, I will make sure they are prosecuted to the extent of the law."

"Well, Evan, I appreciate that, but we already have seven in custody." Sloan didn't say anything else for a second, as if letting his words sink in. The change in Evan's mood soaked over her quickly as his mouth formed a frown, his eyes narrowing before it was replaced quickly with an emotionless stare. That was very telling.

"Oh, is that so." Evan's friendly smile slipped. "Well, like I said, you turn them over to the authorities and I will make sure they get the max prison term. After a fair trial, of course. I'm pretty good at what I do."

"This is VC jurisdiction, and we are also very good at what we do, but thanks." Sloan sounded anything but grateful.

Evan's cool demeanor seemed to slip a little, giving him an anxious edge as the skin around his mouth tightened visibly. Becky knew Sloan was saying things on purpose. She was witnessing her boss in action and he was damn good.

"Well, I have another function that can't wait. It was nice meeting you, Sloan Murphy." Evan nodded toward him, then looked around at Becky. "Ms. Spencer. I'm sure I'll be seeing you both soon."

"You can bet on it," Sloan said as Evan walked away, but Becky thought she was the only one who heard until Evan turned to glance at him.

"Is something wrong?" the mayor asked, his confusion plain on his face.

"Definitely," Sloan replied, finally looking away from where Evan had disappeared. He took Becky's hand and headed toward the door.

Before she knew what was happening, she was inside the limo and Sloan was on the phone. Actually, it was a phone he'd pulled out of a backpack on the floor of the limo. It looked like a disposable cell phone. He looked up at her as he waited for whoever to answer, and she gave him a smile.

She was disappointed, but hoped it didn't show. This wasn't a real date. It was work and that was exactly what he was doing. Working.

"Put me on a secure line." Sloan's voice filled the limo. Again he waited, not saying anything. "Good. I just met Evan Nico, our new DA."

Becky looked down at her dress and straightened it, not that it mattered now. But she didn't want to seem nosey and she definitely didn't want to look disappointed.

"Yeah, no shit," Sloan was saying. "This is going to be tricky. He knows that I know something, which is fine. I want the fucker looking over his shoulder every second. And I think we need to have a little talk with our mayor. Yeah, George is the one who introduced us, very happily I might add. So this Nico asshole has made some definite friends with the higher ups."

Looking out the window, Becky watched the scenery go by, wishing she could have danced with Sloan just once.

"This is why I don't do relationships."

Wondering why Sloan would be saying that to someone on the phone had her looking his way, but he wasn't on the phone anymore. He was staring at her.

"Why are you saying that?" Becky tilted her head. "This was work and hopefully whatever you found out tonight helps you. And the sooner you get on it the better, I'm sure. I totally understand."

Sloan chuckled. "No, actually, I don't think you do. That bastard, Evan Nico, is behind the bombing at the gym, or at least that's what the informants said and what Adam discovered while reading them. His name came up with all of them." Sloan leaned back. "I didn't leave to do more work because there is nothing I can do at the moment anyway. We left because of your safety."

"My safety?" Becky's head snapped back.

"Yes, your safety, which is very important to me," Sloan said as he pushed a button, lowering the privacy window separating them from the driver. "Hank, can you do a twenty-minute drive, then head to my address please?"

"Yes, sir," the man responded before Sloan hit the bottom, shutting the window once more.

"I think we have some unfinished business." He crooked his finger at her.

Becky cocked her eyebrow, her insides going absolutely crazy to the point she felt like there was an earthquake inside her. "I thought you didn't believe in twenty-minute fucks?" Okay, she couldn't believe she'd said that, but seeing the wide smile on Sloan's face and the fire in his eyes, she sure was glad she had.

"I don't." He reached over and pulled her onto his lap. "This is to get you ready for what I'm going to do to you as soon as I have you in my bed."

"Oh, God," she whispered, her body quivering.

"I plan on hearing that a lot tonight." Sloan took her mouth, demanding everything that she was willing to give. She was willing to give it all.

******

Sloan had never tasted anything sweeter than her mouth. She was addictive. He had felt so bad knowing she was excited about the party, yet because of his world, they'd had to leave. There was no way he would have stayed and put her in danger. If it had been just him, he would have investigated a little longer. But Evan Nico was a smart man, that much had been obvious. He'd known he had to take his leave once he'd realized Sloan was on to him.

Sloan was definitely going to make it up to her, starting immediately. His mouth worked from hers to her neck, down to her cleavage. He loved the feel of her fingers in his hair. His pulled the dark purple dress low, exposing one breast, and feasted on the large rosy nipple. He bent and licked, then blew, watching her react to him. A woman's body was amazing; Becky's body was absolutely perfect. He worked her nipple with his tongue, teeth, and lips as his other hand pulled handfuls of her dress fabric out of his way.

His hand slid slowly up her silk-soft legs, his rough fingers a marked contrast. Once he reached his sweet destination, she opened for him. Every male instinct he possessed reared its head in triumph. The wetness that met his eager fingers had him roaring inside. She was more than ready for him. Leaving her breast, he found her mouth to absorb any noise she was about to make as he penetrated her.

Her hands were frantic, as was her body. She was damn tight, the knowledge made him harder, if that were at all possible. His fangs elongated and he wanted nothing more than to taste her—as a man, and as a vampire.

"You're tight," he said against her lips as he worked two fingers inside her. He wanted her ready for him.

She moaned and sensually moved her hips. "It's been a while." Her raspy reply made him smile. "Is twenty minutes up?" Her voice sounded so hopeful he laughed.

"Almost." He began to pump his fingers inside her. "Are you a screamer?"

"I don't know." Her head lay on his arm, her eyes closed in bliss.

"We're about to find out." His voice was harsh with need, his cock harder than it had ever been. He couldn't wait to get her to his apartment. Once there, he may never let her go. And for once in his long life, he was content with that thought.

His thumb found her throbbing nub and he flicked while his fingers pumped. Within seconds she was screaming in his mouth. Oh, she was most definitely a screamer.

He felt the limo slowing and knew they had arrived at his apartment. He continued to kiss Becky, bringing her down from her climax. Pulling away, he smiled into her glassy eyes.

"We're here," he whispered, brushing hair from her eyes.

He helped her sit up and was in the middle of helping fix her dress when there was a tap on his window. He didn't tap back until he was sure Becky was ready.

"Do I... ah...." She cleared her throat as she fluffed her hair, then tugged at her dress, clearly rattled. The she laughed. "Holy shit, I can't even form a rational thought. Let me try that again. Do I look okay?"

She didn't look just okay; she looked well satisfied and he hadn't even started to please her yet. He was glad his tux jacket was long enough to hide his obvious hard-on. "You look more than okay." He smiled when she blushed.

"I don't want to shock poor Hank," Becky teased when Sloan knocked once on the window and the door opened.

Sloan winked at her as he stepped out of the limo, then helped her out. After giving Hank a generous tip, they both thanked the older man and headed inside. The doorman waited with the door already open.

"Good evening, Mr. Murphy. Ma'am." He bowed his head slightly as they went inside.

"Hey, Gary," Sloan greeted without stopping. "How's the wife and kids?"

"Very well, sir." Gary smiled. "Thanks for asking."

He held Becky's hand as they headed toward the elevator. Sloan only nodded to the deskman as they passed. The elevator opened and they walked inside. Sloan hit his floor button, then pulled Becky into his arms, smashing her up against his body to make sure she felt his need for her. When she moaned, he smiled with male pride.

The door opened and he led her to the end of the hallway. Unlocking his door, Sloan held it open for her. When she entered, a content sigh escaped her lips.

"It's beautiful, Sloan," she whispered.

For the first time in a long time, he really looked at his place. Sloan never called it home, because he was never here, but she was right. It was beautiful. A wall of windows overlooked the Ohio River, with double doors opening onto a balcony as long as the apartment.

He leaned against the wall as she strolled to the windows. Becky reached out and opened the doors and stepped outside. Standing at the rail, she raised her face to the sky. Sloan had never seen a more beautiful sight. No other woman had ever been in his apartment, but she looked as if she belonged.

Pushing away from the wall, he flicked on the radio as he made his way toward her. Becky turned at the sound of the music and smiled.

"You know, tonight I had only one regret." She clasped her hands in front of her.

"I can't have that." Sloan stopped inside the door and leaned against it. "What was your one regret?"

"That I didn't get to dance with you," she whispered. Her eyes appeared bright and happy, and the moonlight against her skin made her glow.

Sloan reached out and tugged her into his arms. "If that is your only regret with me, then I'm doing pretty damn well."

They swayed with the music. "I was very proud to be on your arm tonight, Sloan."

"You trying to sweet talk me?" he teased against her hair.

"Yes," she replied, and he felt her smile against his chest.

"Keep going. It's working." They both laughed before they became silent and just swayed in each other's arms, enjoying the music and company.

After a while, Becky pulled away and slipped her shoulder straps down. Her eyes never left his. "I want you, Sloan."

"You're going to have me." He watched as she lowered the dress to her waist, baring her breasts for him. Lowering it further, she slipped it past her gorgeous white lacy thong until it pooled to her feet. She stepped out of the dress, leaving her high heels in place. At that moment he'd never wanted anything more than her. "Every single inch of me."

Chapter 28

Becky stood before him almost completely naked. His words had her crawling up his body. His hands on her bare ass felt so good and sensual, she moaned. They walked through his apartment as she kissed along his neck, lightly biting his ear. She honestly didn't care where he led her, as long as she could feel his naked flesh against hers.

She heard a door shut behind her, but didn't even open her eyes until he began to lower her. She helped him remove his tux jacket, tie, and shirt. His body was strong and toned, with muscles that made her sigh. She ran her fingertips over his chest and across his stomach to his pants. As she unbuttoned his slacks, she leaned forward, putting her mouth on his nipple. His sharp intake of breath told her he liked it, and so did she.

Still in only her heels and thong, she hooked his pants and underwear with her fingers and lowered them, making her breasts rub against his cock as she did. Her eyes feasted on him for only a short second before he grabbed her up with a hiss.

"You are a tease, aren't you?" He growled down at her, his eyes black as night.

"Maybe." She gave him a flirtatious smile before reaching between him and taking his hard cock into her hands. He was not only long, but thick, and damn, it was going to feel so fucking good. Becky closed her eyes, imagining him inside her, over her and taking charge of her body. Just that thought was enough to make her come. She cupped his heavy sac with her other hand and gave him, she hoped, as much pleasure as he had given her in the limo ride.

He caught her hand to stop her. "That's enough." His demand was spoken harshly, full of need.

He kissed his way down her body, and kneeling before her he turned her around and spread her legs apart. She glanced down over her shoulder to see him staring at her ass.

"Jesus." His hands cupped both cheeks before he removed her thong. "I have never seen anything sexier in my life and believe me, I've been alive for a long fucking time."

His words warmed her heart, her body, her soul. It has been so long since any man had showed her any affection and she was eating it up word by word, touch by touch.

Slowly, he bent her forward. "Put your hands on her knees," he instructed, not as harsh as before, but she didn't care if he was. Becky happily obliged. While his hand rested on her lower back, his fingers played with her entrance. There was no need for any type of foreplay; she was so wet and ready she wanted to scream.

"I am going to go slow," Sloan said as his fingers penetrated her. "You are ready for me, but so tight and I don't want to hurt you."

Becky pushed herself back on his fingers, desperate for him to fill her. She was past caring if it was going to hurt. She wanted him and wanted him now. Finally, she felt his cock press against her and tried to quickly push herself on him, but he stopped her with a slap to her ass.

"Dammit, Becky." He smacked her again. "Let me get you used to me and then you can ride me as fast and hard as you want, but you push back one more time, I'm going to blister that ass."

She had moaned when he had spanked her ass. She'd never thought she would have liked that kind of thing, but apparently with Sloan she wanted more, and considered pushing back again just have him smack her ass again.

"You're driving me crazy." She cried out as he pushed inside her, inch by glorious inch.

"You don't even know how fucking hard this is." Sloan was far enough inside that he took her hips into his hands. "But let me tell you one thing. As soon as you are fit for me, I am going to fuck your pussy raw."

"Oh my God!" she cried out, wiggling her ass.

"Told you I'd be hearing that a lot tonight." Sloan growled, pumping his hips in short bursts, working his way inside her.

Her need to come was so strong that she moved her hand to take care of herself, but Sloan stopped her. "Please."

"Don't you fucking touch anything but your knees," he ordered, then smacked her ass again. "I'm in control and I tell you when you come, and when you do, it will be by my hand only."

Finally, he worked his cock all the way inside her and she wanted to scream in relief and agony, but not because it hurt. Instead, she needed him to fuck her.

His hand ran up her back to her hair and he grabbed a handful, pulling her head back. It wasn't rough and it didn't hurt, but it made her tingling worse because it turned her on.

"Are you ready?" he whispered close to her ear. "Because I'm going to fuck you good, Becky."

"Oh, God!" she cried out, her pussy tightening around him in anticipation. He wrapped his arm around her waist as he pulled out of her. "No!"

He chuckled as he picked her up and carried her to the bed, laid her down, and tugged her toward the edge. The bed was high, high enough for him to push inside her without climbing on the bed. They both stilled as their eyes met. Finally, Becky reached up and touched his face.

"I think I've been waiting for you my whole life." She said the words she felt in her heart, consequences be damned. If he rejected her, it would break her, but at least he knew what she felt in that moment.

He closed his eyes for a second, but penetrated her fully and stopped. She sucked in air, her eyes closing in pleasure.

"You are my whole life." His whispered words rushed over her as he began to move inside her. She held on to those words, cherished them for later when things would change, as they always did.

Silently, they enjoyed each other's bodies, giving each other pleasure, and he was absolutely right. Sloan definitely didn't believe in a twenty-minute fuck. She knew she was close again. Yes, again. He had brought her to climax twice already, yet he still continued. Sloan had picked her up and fucked her against the wall. He'd also fucked her against no wall, just using his strength to move her up and down his thick cock, and they were since back on the bed.

His eyes were completely black and his fangs dipped over his lower lip. Becky couldn't stop staring at them. She wanted to feel their bite. She was afraid to ask, but she wanted it more than anything.

"Sloan," she whispered as she rocked against him. His eyes found hers, his hand going to her cheek, down her neck to her breast to pinch her nipple. But his eyes remained on hers, waiting for her to continue. But she chickened out, afraid to ask.

"What is it, Becky?" He slowed, his eyes questioning.

She shook her head. "Nothing." She reached up, but he pulled away.

"Never tell me nothing when I know you want something." Sloan gave her a hard thrust. "What do you want?"

Swallowing hard, she reached up and touched the tip of his fang. Understanding lit his eyes.

"Are you sure?" he asked, his cock growing harder inside her.

She moaned and wiggled her hips underneath him at the sensation of him growing inside her. "Never been more sure." She smiled up at him.

Sloan groaned, his eyes closing for a second before opening again to see Becky had exposed her neck for him, but she could still see him. Opening his mouth, he lowered until the tip of his fangs raked erotically along her skin.

She had to admit, she was a little scared, but no way in hell would she back out. Becky wanted this and after the sharp pain of his fangs penetrated her tender skin, she was damn glad she'd asked because the tug of his lips mixed with the stinging pain sent her over the edge, and he quickly followed. It was mind-blowing and something she would never forget. She prayed she would have the chance to feel it again.

******

Sloan stood on the balcony wearing a pair of old workout sweats. Becky had fallen asleep after their third round of sex. It was five in the morning and he stood alone, staring out over the waking city.

He anxiously waited for her to wake, hoping he'd see no regret in her eyes. For the first time in his life, he was afraid and he didn't fucking like it. He was determined to lay down his faults before her, because if there was going to be a relationship between them, he needed Becky to enter with eyes wide open to who he really was.

Leaning on the rail, he heard her before she made her presence known. It was time. Time to let her know what she had gotten herself into.

"Hey, you." Her voice was raspy as she walked up behind him.

Sloan turned and groaned. She wore his white tux shirt and nothing else. Her hair was messy and her eyes sleepy and sexy. He couldn't help it. He pulled her into his arms, putting his chin on top of her head.

"What are you doing out here?" She glanced up at him, then yawned.

"Just thinking," he replied, hesitating.

"About what?" She ran her hand across his stomach. When he didn't answer, she looked up at him again. "Sloan?"

"Listen." Sloan stopped when she pushed away from him.

"Wow, really?" She stood before him, not caring that his shirt spread open, showing her breasts and pussy. "You couldn't wait a few more hours before telling me how this isn't going to work?"

"What?" Sloan's eyes narrowed.

"Too bad for you, because you could have gotten another fuck out of me," she said, then turned away. Hastily, he grabbed her before she could take a step. "Seriously, what is wrong with me? This is—"

Sloan shut her up by smashing his mouth against hers. At first she started to fight him, but within seconds, she was pressed against him. When she eased into the kiss and surrendered herself to him, he pulled his mouth away.

"Shut up," he ordered before she could start again. When she started to speak, he raised his eyebrow at her. "First off, there is absolutely nothing wrong with you."

"Then—" She shut up at his look. "Sorry, go on."

"I have been standing out here for an hour trying to decide exactly how I'm going to let you go if you decide to walk away." Sloan's voice was even and strong. "But I want you to walk into this with your eyes wide open. I'm not an easy man. I have more responsibilities than ten men put together. I'm a prick. I have a short temper. I—"

"I'm not running." Becky stopped him. "So you're wasting your breath. Whatever you say—unless you tell me you don't want me—will not send me running."

"You'll never hear those words," Sloan assured her. "What I do is dangerous, but I promise you I will keep you safe."

"I have no doubt." Becky reached out and touched his cheek. "I trust you. You're a good man, Sloan Murphy, but I promise not to tell."

Sloan smiled, pulling her toward him. "Now, about that fuck."

Becky walked behind him to the rail. Grabbing hold of it, she spread her legs, then looked at him over her shoulder, giving him a sexy grin. "Ready when you are, Warrior."

"Jesus." Sloan was there in a flash and buried deep inside her within seconds. "I may not survive you, but it sure is going to be fun trying."

Chapter 29

Katrina let herself in Becky's house. She didn't know when or if she would be home tonight. Blaze had walked in with her.

"Thanks for bringing me," Katrina said as she put her bag on the floor next to the door.

"What time is Becky coming home?" Blaze leaned against the wall.

"Not sure." Katrina frowned, her hand going to her stomach. "She may not even come home tonight, but if she doesn't, I can always catch a cab to training."

The bar across the street was busy. People stood outside talking loudly. Their drunken chatter rose above the music playing inside.

"Do you need to feed?" His eyes were on her hand that sat on her stomach.

"No," she lied, but when his eyes rose to meet hers, she sighed. "I can't keep taking your blood. I'm fine."

"You're newly turned, Katrina." Blaze closed the door, shutting out some of the noise. "You're going to need to feed more frequently than anyone else at least for another month."

"Then let me feed you." Katrina immediately wanted to crawl in a hole and die. Why in the hell had she said that?

Blaze actually smiled. "Now that would be defeating the purpose of me feeding you, wouldn't it?"

Katrina nodded. "I just feel bad."

"Well, don't." Blaze took his shirt off and tossed it on the couch. He walked into the kitchen. "Come on, hop on the counter."

Doing as he said, she hopped up, which gave her the perfect height. Staring at his neck, she licked her lips. His blood was addictive. She craved it, and that scared her. His was the only blood she'd tasted and she wondered if anyone else's would taste as good. She didn't know the answer to that and wanted to ask, but didn't dare.

It was always awkward at first. She wanted to touch him, but always hesitated. Blaze moved between her legs. He leaned into her and tilted his head, giving her easy access to the vein in his neck. Slowly, she lowered her mouth, making sure her fangs were over the vein before she gently sank her teeth into his skin.

Her tongue pressed against his neck as she tugged at the vein, taking his spicy blood into her mouth. Her nipples hardened and her private area tingled. She wasn't totally naïve. She knew all about sex between a man and a woman. She knew she wanted him and every time she took his blood, she wanted more. Katrina had also seen his reaction after. She had seen the hard bulge in his jeans as he'd walk away from her; she had even seen him adjust himself, which made her tingle and throb even more.

As she took more of his blood, she wondered if she offered herself to him, would he take her or reject her. Taking a chance, she put her hand on the other side of his neck, her touch gentle, letting it run along his jaw.

Abruptly, he grabbed her hand and moved it away. She pulled her mouth from his neck, licking the wound closed. With downcast eyes, she felt embarrassment heat her cheeks; her touch had been rejected. She should have known.

"I'm sorry," Katrina said, her voice low as she wiped her mouth.

Blaze lifted her face to his. "You did nothing wrong," he responded, his eyes black as they stared into hers. "When taking blood, sometimes feelings get involved. It's normal."

"It is?" She knew she sounded relieved, and she was.

"Yeah." He smiled, but his smiles always looked so sad.

"Thank you for…." Katrina stopped what she was about to say and hopped down off the counter.

"For what?" Blaze walked over to get his shirt and put it back on.

"For being nice to me," she replied, crossing her arms and leaning against the refrigerator.

Staring out of the window, Blaze didn't respond. "Are you afraid to stay here alone?"

"No, I'm fine." Katrina shrugged, but he couldn't see her. "I'm used to it."

That did make him turn around. "What happened with you, Katrina?"

It was her turn to give a sad smile and a shake of her head. "That's not something I'll discuss with anyone."

"We'll see about that," Blaze said, then headed toward the door. "Everyone needs someone to talk to."

"Yes, I guess *we* do," Katrina called him out. "Guess we're both two lost souls."

"I know exactly where I am," he replied, before walking out. "Make sure you lock this door."

"Thank you again, Blaze." But he was already on his bike and riding out.

******

Blaze went around the block, then stopped far enough away from Becky's to keep an eye on the place and the bar. He wasn't comfortable leaving Katrina there alone and until the bar closed or Becky came home, he was keeping an eye out. He should be patrolling, but that could wait.

Katrina was a vampire, but she was a kind soul. The word soul made him think of what she'd said before he'd left. She was right, but no way in hell would he admit it, at least to her. She was coming around slowly and would make a good warrior. He smiled at the thought of her with Steve today. Now that was hilarious, but she'd been ready to stand up for Steve. He'd known what it would take for her to come out of her shell: helping someone she cared about or an animal from danger, or even supporting someone who needed help.

With a sigh, Blaze crossed his arms as he straddled his bike. His feelings for Katrina were complicated and he hoped to hell they got straightened out and soon. He wasn't there for a half an hour before some drunk ass started stumbling out of the bar and toward the road. A stray dog he had noticed earlier was snooping around and went to sniff the man's shoes. The drunk asshole kicked out toward the dog.

"Shit!" Blaze started his bike as soon as he saw Becky's door fly open. Katrina flew down the steps.

She yelled at the man while the dog limped toward her. The man yelled back at her, his arms waving all around. As Katrina leaned down to grab the dog, she took her eyes off the man and didn't notice he had raised his foot to kick again, this time hitting Katrina in the side of the head. She fell backwards onto the concrete, smacking her head hard. Blaze's loud growl of rage and the sound of his bike alerted the drunk, but it was too late. As Blaze rode between him and Katrina, Blaze kicked his foot out, hitting the man in the chest, sending him flying.

Turning, he parked his bike quickly and ran to Katrina, who sat up and searched for the dog, who was sitting on Becky's front porch.

"Are you okay?" Blaze helped her up.

"Yeah," Katrina replied, looking around. "Where is he?"

"He's on the porch, Katrina." Blaze snapped, then rolled his eyes when she took off toward the dog.

"What the hell?" a man yelled, running to the drunk. "What did you do to Bob?"

Blaze turned to see the bar emptying out onto the street. "Katrina, lock the door and get on my bike, now!"

A man headed toward his bike, but Blaze sneered at him, showing his fangs. "Big mistake, asshole."

"Holy shit," one man said, backing up. "He's a fucking vampire."

"He kicked me for no reason." Bob was up on his feet now, actually sounding a little more sober as he pointed toward Blaze.

"That's a lie!" Katrina shouted, heading toward Blaze's bike. "You kicked this poor dog, asshole." Katrina climbed on Blaze's bike, holding the dog close.

"Katrina," Blaze warned, his eyes tracking everyone before he addressed them. "You have two choices, one good and one bad. The good choice is to turn away and walk back into that bar."

"What's the bad choice," the man who had found Bob first shouted.

Blaze smiled, his eyes swirling fire. "Not picking the good one."

"He's only one," another guy, whose whiskey was talking for him, shouted. "We can take one vampire."

Blaze looked his way and smiled. "You want to bet your life on that?"

That shut whiskey boy up real quick.

"So any takers, or are we just going to stand here all night and talk about it?" Blaze eyed the crowd. He could take them, he knew, but Katrina sat unprotected holding a fucking dog.

"I say we don't mess with this fucker," another drunk who was closer said. "Look at his eyes. Something's not right with him."

"That's the smartest thing I've heard any of you say since this shit started." Blaze backed toward his bike.

"Call the cops!" Bob yelled as he staggered. "I'm pressing charges."

"And I'm pressing charges against you for animal cruelty." Katrina once again threatened.

Keeping an eye on the crowd, he gave them a smile. "The name's Blaze." He nodded to Bob, then started his bike, revved it up, and took off.

Blaze was glad he'd left without having to tackle twenty or so men on his own. Not that it would have been a problem, but his concern was Katrina.

"I think he needs to go to a vet," Katrina hollered over the sound of the engine.

"Are you fucking serious?" Blaze slowed to a stop.

"Yeah, there's an emergency vet on Vine." He heard the dog whimpering. "Please, Blaze."

"Son of a bitch!" Blaze cursed as he turned his bike around and headed toward Vine. "Well, this night just keeps getting better and better."

Chapter 30

Sloan couldn't keep his mind on what he was doing. Every few seconds he looked at Becky, who was busy at her desk. They had spent the whole morning in and out of bed deciding to come in to work at around noon. It was almost one. He had called a meeting with all the Warriors about Evan Nico.

At five till one, they all started filing into his office. He had already let Becky know about the bet, so she wouldn't be shocked or upset. He was more pissed than she was about the whole betting issue. She just laughed it off with a shrug. He continued to look busy, but the silent Warriors drew his attention because a silent Warrior in this group spelled trouble.

Lifting his head, his eyes met a grinning Jared's. Sid sat in front of him, his feet for once not on his desk. Leaning back in his chair, Sloan continued his observation, and every single one of them was staring at him expectantly. Finally, his eyes met Becky's. She also stared at him over her computer screen and a fucking grin just popped out on his face. *Fuck!*

"I knew it!" Sid sat up in his chair and pointed at Sloan. "I fucking knew it."

"Sid, you don't know shit." Sloan growled, his eyes narrowing dangerously.

"Oh, yeah." Jared rubbed his hands together. "The boss man got laid."

"Watch yourself, Jared." Sloan edged forward in warning.

"Sorry, Becky," Jared called back to Becky. The huge grin on his face stayed in place.

Becky glanced up from her computer and smirked. "It's fine, Jared."

"See, she can take it without getting all pissed off." Jared gave her a nod.

"You're right, you know." Becky glanced at Sloan, who winked at her. "The boss man got laid, got laid *real* good."

Everyone turned to look at her with various stages of shock registering on their faces.

"I was out with your mates the other day." Becky stood, walking toward them. "And I think maybe, just maybe, you might want to pay more attention to, well you know, than you do your boss's... you know."

A few chuckles filled the silence and it wasn't Jared or Sid who were chuckling.

"No, I don't fucking know." Jared narrowed his eyes on her as she passed him and walked around Sloan's desk.

"And that's the problem." Becky gave him a sad look. She was sure everyone could see her poor attempt at hiding a grin.

Sloan wrapped his arm around her waist as she bent down to kiss him, then whispered something to him and walked toward the door.

"Good thing she wasn't talking to me," Sid mumbled, not throwing jokes around.

"Oh, but I was." She gave him a smile. Before Becky closed the door, she peeked back in. "Don't fuck with a redhead." She gave them both a wink before shutting the door.

Laughter filled the room, Sloan's the loudest. "You should have seen your face." Sloan grinned. "How does it feel, assholes?"

"My woman is well satisfied," Jared announced, rolling his shoulders.

"She's a good fit for you." Damon, who didn't say much ever, had a huge grin on his face. "Because that was some good shit."

"So are you mated?" Sid also grinned, indicating Becky had impressed him with her sass.

Sloan looked around at everyone. They were his men, his team, and they deserved to know. As much as he closed his personal shit from anyone, Becky was something he didn't want to hide. She deserved better than that. He couldn't quite believe how strong his feelings were for her, but they was there and he couldn't deny it. Didn't want to deny it.

"Not yet," Sloan replied, still feeling strange sharing his feelings.

"You better hurry before someone snatches her up," Jill warned with everyone agreeing.

"No one will touch her." Sloan growled, his protective instinct in overdrive. He quickly calmed himself, aware he was overreacting. "I want to meet and talk to her son first."

"Awww." Jill sighed. "How sweet."

Rolling his eyes, Sloan was done with the conversation, and he was far from fucking sweet. He was a prick. "Shut it, Jill," Sloan warned before handing her photographs to hand out to everyone. "We have more important shit to deal with right now. Where in the fuck is Steve?" Sloan asked, looking around.

"It's about damn time someone noticed I was missing." Steve's voice echoed in the room as a picture was snatched out of Jill's hand and floated around the room.

Sloan looked around as everyone watched. Jared and Sid shook their heads. Suddenly Steve appeared in front of his desk.

"Ta-fucking-da!" Steve had his arms outstretched like he had just done the best magic trick in the world. "So? What do you think? It's my power. I become invisible."

"No shit." Sloan sighed, leaning back in his chair staring at the kid. It was going to be a fucking mess. Steve with such a power was scary at best, and he knew for a fact someone in this room was going to kick the kid's ass for fucking with them, and he was going to make damn sure it wasn't him. "I'm going to tell you this right now. You listening?"

Steve's smile faded slightly, his arms dropped. "Yes, I'm listening."

"Although this power you have acquired is probably one of the best so far because of the shit we can do with it, if you ever and I mean ever try to fuck with me, I will kill you." Sloan held up his hand before Steve's mouth opened. "No. Think about this, Steve. I know you very well, probably better than yourself. This power can get you killed by your peers. Us. Do not and I repeat, *do not* fuck with me ever. Understood."

"Ah, so did this time count?" Steve looked a little afraid, his voice shaky.

"You got a free pass this time." Seeing the disappointed look on his face, Sloan actually felt bad for being so hard on the kid. Fuck, he was getting soft. "And be ready on a moment's notice because this power is going to come in very handy and be used a lot."

"Sweet!" Steve did a tame version of the fist pump, then passed Jill. "My power's better than yours, biotch," he whispered, but everyone heard.

Jill used her power to slide a chair in front of Steve as he passed, making him trip. "Might want to rethink that, asshole." Jill smiled as she continued handing out the photos.

Sloan seriously wondered how in the hell they ever got anything done. These guys fucked off more than they.... No, that wasn't true. He had the best team and he knew it, but he'd never let them know that. He'd never live that shit down with his crew.

"This is Evan Nico, who I happened to meet last night." Sloan decided to let the shit pass and concentrate on what needed to be done.

Everyone stared down at the image Jill had handed out.

"He's the new DA," Sloan continued. "We all know that the main name that came out during the interrogation was Evan Nico."

"What happened to Lance?" Damon asked, his eyes rising from the photo.

"Busted for heroin," Duncan answered, handing out the police report.

"That's bullshit." Damon stared down at the paper. "I've known Lance for years. He didn't do heroin and he sure as hell didn't sell the shit."

"He was framed." Sloan nodded in agreement. "And in steps Evan Nico. Too coincidental. Nico is a slick player. He isn't too happy that we have seven of his thugs in our custody. He wanted me to turn them over."

"We got everything out of them that we can anyway." Duncan eyed Sloan. "Let him have them. Save us money on feeding the fuckers."

"How in the hell did he get into the DA position?" Sid frowned, totally focused and serious.

"Governor appointed him," Duncan replied, his eyes narrowed. "After Sloan called me last night, I did some checking and it seems this asshole has a lot of connections with some important people. This isn't going to go away overnight, unless a pile of evidence pointing directly at Evan Nico falls in our laps."

"What do you think his purpose is?" Jared asked, looking first to

Duncan and then Sloan.

The front door buzzer sounded and they all looked up at the monitor. "Ah, looks like we're about to find out." Sloan's grin spread across his face, but didn't quite reach his eyes. Evan Nico stood on their doorstep with three uniformed police officers. "This should be entertaining. Let them in, Damon."

******

Becky headed into the kitchen with a smile. Jared and Sid totally deserved some of what they were dishing out. Pouring a cup of coffee, she hoped to hell it was strong. She was dead on her feet, but it was totally worth it. With a satisfied sigh, she walked out of the kitchen with her much-needed coffee.

With Sloan on her mind, it took her a minute to realize who was following Damon to Sloan's office.

"Ms. Spencer." Evan Nico smiled at her. "How nice to see you again. Actually, I didn't expect to see you here at all."

Okay, she definitely didn't like this guy. He tried way too hard to be nice and that triggered warning bells. This man was far from nice.

"I'm the secretary, Mr. Nico." Becky didn't respond with, "nice to see you also" because she was never much of a liar. "Why wouldn't I be here?"

"Oh, I thought...." His eyes roamed down her body, a heat that made her very uncomfortable filling his eyes.

"You thought wrong." She wasn't about to let this asshole know anything about her and Sloan. Damon suddenly stepped between them, blocking Evan from her view.

"Through that door right there." Damon nodded, his tone stern and downright mean.

Becky followed, wondering what in the hell was going on. Once inside, she went to her desk and sat down. Her eyes went directly to Sloan and the half smile on his face sent shivers down her spine. She was about to see Sloan at work. His smile was not a welcoming one. This man was the real Sloan Murphy.

Chapter 31

Sloan didn't even stand when Evan and his posse of, if he guessed right, dirty cops walked into his office. As soon as his eyes met Evan's, he knew as confident as Evan tried to appear, he was intimidated and that suited Sloan just fine.

"What can I do for you, Nico?" Sloan used his last name purposely. Self-important assholes usually liked formal and this fucker would never get the respect of formal from him. Best he learned that now.

Sure enough, the frown on the bastard's face indicated he was not happy being addressed that way.

"It's Evan," he tried to correct, but Sloan wasn't having it.

"I know," was Sloan's only reply.

"Do you have a problem with me?" Evan glanced around at all the Warriors staring at him, before looking back at Sloan. "Because that is going to make it very difficult for us to work together."

"Actually, yes, I do." Sloan was going to lay it all on the table. Might as well let him know what he was in for, because it was going to be a long, miserable time for him if he decided to go up against the VC. "And I don't see us working well together. I believe Lance Garfield, who is well respected by each Warrior here, was framed. We are going to make it our priority to investigate and clear his name. I believe you are in this position under false pretenses and I also believe you are behind the recent bombings of the Warrior training facilities, mine included."

Sloan had to give him credit. Evan didn't flinch, but Sloan was trained to spot weakness and he saw a flicker of fear in the man's eyes before it was replaced with anger. "You best watch yourself. I could sue you for slander."

"You could, if I was wrong." Sloan cocked his eyebrow at him. "But we both know I'm not. So why don't you tell me why you dragged your suit-wearing ass down here for before I have my Warriors kick you and your thug cops out of my office and off my property."

"You don't know who you are dealing with." Evan leaned toward Sloan, but far enough away to be safe.

Sloan stood quickly, making Evan and the cops take a step back. "I know exactly who I'm dealing with and if you think you have any power over me, then you don't know who you are dealing with."

Everyone was on edge, waiting. Sloan knew exactly where Becky was just in case shit went bad. Damon glanced at him, then to Becky, and positioned himself ready to protect her if he needed. Sloan gave him a short nod.

"Now, why don't you tell me why you are here so you can get the fuck out?" Sloan sneered, already done with the game of who had the bigger dick. He had no doubts about himself, but Evan did, and he could see it in his eyes.

"I have an arrest warrant for Blaze." Evan tossed the warrant on Sloan's desk from where he stood.

Sloan looked to Blaze who looked bored, but ready to defend if needed. Picking up the warrant, Sloan read it. "And what exactly did he do?"

"He beat up an upstanding citizen in the community who is pressing charges," Evan replied, nodding toward one of the officers who went toward Blaze, who still looked bored.

"You take one more step, I will have one of my Warriors toss your ass out." Sloan didn't even take his eyes off the warrant before looking up at Blaze.

"I dropped Katrina off last night," Blaze answered Sloan's silent question. "As I was keeping an eye out, because I didn't trust leaving her there alone, upstanding Bob came stumbling out of the bar."

Sloan's eyes went to Evan, who tugged at his tie. His focus then returned to Blaze. He sent a silent message to Jill to get Katrina. She left immediately.

"He made his way into the street, probably trying to find where he parked his car so he could drive home drunk, but instead, he kicked a dog that I spent the whole fucking night at the vet's with." Blaze glared at Evan. "Katrina must have been looking out the window and ran out. Before I could get to them, upstanding Bob once again kicked out, but instead of the dog, he kicked Katrina on the side of the head. So I repaid him with a kick to the chest from my bike as I passed."

"Nice." Sid nodded at Blaze.

"That's not the story I was told." Evan didn't look very confident.

"Of course it wasn't, asshole." Blaze laughed. "I bet you have, let's see, twenty witnesses saying something different. I bet it was the same drunk-ass punks who came out of the bar to stand up for upstanding Bob, and were trying to decide whether to jump me and Katrina."

The door opened and Katrina walked in, her eyes going directly to the cops and then to Blaze.

"Katrina, what happened last night?" Sloan asked just as Jill closed the door.

Sloan stood and listened to the exact same story that Blaze just replayed, but from Katrina's lips.

"And I want to press charges of animal cruelty," Katrina ended, her eyes going to the cops and then Evan. "Do I do that with you?"

The Warriors chuckled, shaking their heads. Evan looked embarrassed and pissed.

"None of that matters, little girl, and if you know what's good for you, you'll shut your mouth." Evan pointed to the warrant. "I am taking him in and there is nothing you can do about it. It's legal. And I know he's not a Warrior so you have no jurisdiction on the matter."

"Seems like you know an awful lot about my men for a DA." Sloan smirked. He also knew for a fact he did have jurisdiction, but before he could say anything, Blaze walked up to Sloan's desk.

"Give me the fucking paper." Blaze's eyes swirled fire.

"Are you sure?" Sloan wanted this, but he didn't want Blaze to feel forced.

"I know you have it all ready to go, Sloan." Blaze's eyes narrowed at him. "Just give me the fucking paper before I change my mind."

Sloan looked back at Becky, who was already at the file cabinet. She handed Damon a file, which he handed to Jared, who in turn handed it to Sloan. Pulling out the paper, he laid it on his desk in front of Blaze. Without hesitation, Blaze picked up a pen and signed without even looking it over.

Blaze tossed the pen down and then grabbed the warrant and smacked it none too lightly on Evan's chest. "Stay out of my fucking way. And if you ever talk to her like that again, I'll burn your ass alive," Blaze warned him before he walked back to his place, crossed his arms, and once again looked bored.

"I won't forget that threat." Evan eyed Blaze with hate.

"That would be healthy for you," Blaze responded, no emotion whatsoever in his voice or expression.

Evan looked at the paper on Sloan's desk. "What is that?"

"He is now an official VC Warrior." Sloan grabbed the pen and signed underneath Blaze's name. "And I just witnessed it."

"This offense happened before he signed that paper, making it void and my warrant legal," Evan spat, showing his true colors.

Sloan picked up the paper and held it up. "Seems it was dated a month ago."

"This is bullshit and against the law." Evan huffed, then looked at his officers. "I have witnesses."

"Which reminds me." Sloan grabbed a pen and paper, tossing it to Duncan. "Get their names and badge numbers."

"What for?" Evan's anger simmered a little.

"Listen, Nico. I'm done with answering your questions." Sloan leaned toward him, his eyes narrowing in anger. "How about you answer some of mine? How did you set up Lance Garfield, because we both know that's exactly what happened in order for you to get his position. Here's another one for you, while you try to think your way out of that one, what is your aim in trying to take down the VC trainee program?"

"You don't know who you're de—" Evan started to say, but Sloan stopped him.

"Dealing with." Sloan finished for him. "You better get a better vocabulary when dealing with me, asshole, because you already said that. Your first mistake was trying to injure or kill under my watch. Your second mistake was walking into my house and trying to tell me what to do. Your third mistake is still standing here. Get the fuck out and don't come back."

"This isn't over." He pointed at Sloan. "Not by a long shot."

"No, it's not, but it will be me that finishes." Sloan sat down and leaned back in his chair with his arms crossed. "I've been doing this since before you were born, motherfucker, and I'll be damned if I let a snot-nosed silver-spoon piece of shit take me or mine down. You drew the line and I've jumped over that son of a bitch. Now I'm not big on repeating myself, so I'll have my Warriors escort you and your thugs out of my house."

Duncan handed Sloan the cops' names and badge numbers before Jared and Sid, followed by the rest, escorted them out of the room. Evan shouted threats the whole way. Blaze was the last to leave.

"Blaze, we can tear this up." Sloan held out Blaze's official oath.

Blaze stopped, his eyes going from the paper to Sloan. "And that right there is the reason I won't. You're a decent man, Sloan. I just hope you don't regret that paper in your hand." Blaze shut the door behind him.

Sloan sighed, then sat back in his chair, his eyes closed. Something hit his lap, making his eyes pop open. Becky sat on his lap, her eyes focused on his.

"Are you okay?" She ran a finger from his forehead to his chin, then kissed him softly.

"I am now." He held her close. "Just part of the job."

"Actually, you were pretty hot." Becky gave him a sexy grin. "Getting all angry and besting that asshole. Definitely hot!"

"Ah, you think so, do you?" Sloan kissed her neck. "I have enemies, Becky, a lot of them, and they keep coming. Are you sure you want this?"

"I've never been more sure in my life about anything." Becky pulled away, looking him straight in the eye. "But I have a small problem."

Sloan's eyes narrowed, not liking that at all. "What?"

"I think I'm in love with my boss," Becky whispered, her eyes hopeful.

Never in his life had he felt this emotion. His throat actually tightened up. Glancing away from her, Sloan had to get his shit together before he started crying like a bitch. Sloan Murphy didn't fucking cry. Clearing his throat, he looked back. "That's too bad, because I'm in love with you and I'm Sloan, not your boss."

Becky did cry. Her eyes overflowed as she crawled further up his lap, holding his neck tightly, her tears wetting his neck. After a few minutes, she pulled away. "Thank you so much."

Sloan actually laughed. "What in the hell are you thanking me for?" He wiped her tears.

"For showing me that I am loveable." Becky's voice cracked. "Because honestly, I was really doubting."

"I will one day kick your ex's ass." Sloan growled. "Never doubt that I love you, Becky. I never thought it was possible and I denied it would ever happen, but it has and you are mine. And tonight, I will show you exactly how lovable you are."

His hand reached behind her head as he smashed his mouth against hers.

"I fucking knew it." Jared popped in the office with Sid and the rest following. "Pay up, fuckers!" There was cursing and laughs going around, but Sloan and Becky just stared at each other.

"The bet?" Becky said against his mouth.

"Yes," Sloan replied. "They're assholes."

"Only Sloan can kick ass one minute and have a beautiful woman on his lap the next," Sid said as he sat down across from Becky and Sloan. "I want to be Sloan Murphy when I grow up."

Chapter 32

Sloan was a nervous fucking wreck. Jesus, he could face the meanest, baddest motherfuckers on the planet, but meeting Becky's son was making him nauseous, and he was a vampire. Vampires didn't get fucking nauseous.

"You good?" Becky asked from the seat next to him.

"Yep," he replied, but his stomach said, "Nope."

He knew how important her son was to her and Sloan hoped to hell he didn't blow it. Seeing the restaurant sign, he pulled in. Frankie was visiting with his dad, but had set time to meet and have dinner with Becky and him.

Sloan smiled as Becky leaned forward, her face practically pushed against the windshield. He felt her excitement and mixed with his nerves, it was fucking driving him insane. He did not like this feeling at all, but he would go through the gates of hell for her. Sloan just hoped that wasn't the case today.

"There he is," she shouted and he barely stopped the car before she was jumping out.

"Dammit, Becky!" Sloan shouted, slamming on the brakes. "Wait until I stop." But she was long gone.

Getting out of the car, he hit the lock button and put the keys in his pocket. Sloan walked toward them, but stayed back, giving them their moment. Her son was taller than her, well-built with dark hair that hung to his shoulders. Their eyes met and as always, Sloan could tell by a man's eyes what kind of man he was. Becky's son was a righteous guy who was very protective of his mother. Sloan knew immediately they would get along just fine.

Becky finally let him go and turned toward Sloan. "I'm so sorry." Becky reached toward Sloan, who stepped closer and took her hand.

"Frankie, this is Sloan Murphy. Sloan, this is my son, Frankie."

Reaching out, Sloan shook Frankie's hand. Her son's grip was firm, but not disrespectfully so. "It's nice to finally meet you, Frankie." Sloan smiled down at him. "I've heard a lot about you."

"Oh, God." Frankie glanced at his mom with a look only a son could give his mother. "I can only imagine what she's told you."

"All good." Sloan laughed, enjoying Becky's blush. "I promise."

They made their way inside and got seated. Sloan noticed Frankie glancing at their joined hands, but he didn't mention it.

"So, this is your boss, huh?" Frankie grinned, looking between Becky and Sloan.

"Well, yes, but…." Becky struggled with her words.

"Mom, it's cool." Frankie laughed, his eyes going to Sloan, then back to his mom. "Are you happy?"

"Very." Becky nodded, then wiped a tear that leaked from her eye.

"That's all I want for you." Frankie's eyes misted. "That's all I ever wanted for you, Mom."

"Ugh, now my nose is all runny." She scooted toward Sloan. "Let me run to the restroom real quick."

Sloan stood, then looked for the restroom and around the restaurant. When he felt okay with letting her go, he helped her out of the booth. She wiped another tear away.

"Sorry, I don't know why I'm so damn weepy lately." She gave him a wet smile.

Chuckling, Sloan sat back down and watched her disappear into the restroom before looking back at Frankie, who was staring at him.

"You're a Warrior?" Frankie asked, taking a sip of water.

"Yes," Sloan replied, waiting for the next question.

"Pretty obvious." Frankie smiled. "The way you checked out the place before letting my mom go alone says a lot about you."

"I'm in love with your mom, Frankie." Sloan just came right out and laid it on the table. That was the type of man he was. "I promise you I will take care of her and never do her wrong. She loves you and I respect that. I hope we can be friends, but if not, just know your mom is well taken care of and I will never come between the two of you."

Frankie sat for a long time staring at Sloan. "My dad's an asshole, but I still see him because he holds it over Mom's head if I don't." Frankie glanced over to see if she was coming. "You treat my mom right and we will be the best of friends."

"I plan on kicking your dad's ass one day." Sloan cocked an eyebrow, waiting for Frankie's reaction.

"Just don't kill him and let me be there when you do," Frankie replied, his face serious.

Sloan thought about that for a minute, then nodded. "Deal."

Frankie laughed, giving Sloan a knuckle bump. "You're okay, man."

"What's so funny?" Becky asked as she scooted back in the booth.

Sloan and Frankie just looked at each other. "Guy talk," they both said at the same time.

Enjoying watching Becky and her son interact, while also including him, was something Sloan would never forget. And unfortunately it was over too soon. Frankie had to get back to school and Sloan had things he had to take care of.

The ride was quiet on the way home. Sloan kept glancing over at Becky to check on her, but gave her space. He knew watching Frankie leave broke her heart.

Pulling into an empty parking lot, he put the car in park, then reached for her. She rested her head on his chest, but didn't cry.

"I miss him," Becky whispered. "I know he has to be his own man, but it's so hard."

"You did a great job with him, Becky," Sloan said against her hair as he stared at nothing out the window. "He's going to be a good man."

They stayed like that for a few minutes more before they took off again. She'd needed to be held and he suddenly realized so did he, because what caused her pain, caused him the same.

Instead of going back to the compound, he drove to his apartment. He was glad Becky didn't question it. There was something more important he had to do than work. That thought kind of freaked him out a little because for so long, work was what was most important to him, but that had changed, and fast.

Once upstairs, Becky gave him a kiss, then disappeared on the balcony. He knew she was still missing her son. He felt the same way when she wasn't in his presence.

Heading into his bedroom, he unlocked his safe in his closet and removed a small box. Walking back out, he paused and watched her as she gazed at the river. The view he had on the top floor was magnificent, but with her standing there as part of the view, it was spectacular. She must have sensed him because she turned her head to look at him over her shoulder. Her smile was enough to drop him to his knees.

Instead, he walked toward her, the box clasped in his hand. Reaching out, Sloan turned her around and then dropped to one knee. Opening the box, he turned it toward her. He had bought the ring after their first night together; that was how sure he had been she was his.

"I have never loved before like I love you." Sloan stared into her eyes, which were open wide in shock. "I know this is soon, but I have never been more sure of anything in my life. If you agree to be my wife, I would also ask for you to be my mate in the vampire way. I will never let you down, will love you forever, and I promise I will never break your heart. I'm an asshole, work too much and have some shitty habits, but know I love you and want you by my side for life."

Becky didn't even look at the ring. She just threw herself at him, toppling them over. He broke her fall with his body.

"Will you marry me, Becky Spencer?" Sloan said from his back, the box still in his hand.

"I will marry you, Sloan, and you're not an asshole." She kissed his face all over. "And I'm your secretary, so when I think you're working too hard, I will make you take a break. There're things I've wanted to try in that office and chair and as for your shitty habits, I've a few of my own."

Sloan didn't know how long they lay there, but it was long enough that he was ready to strip her clothes off. "Do you want your ring?" He laughed when she straddled him and gazed at the box.

"Of course, but I've got all I need right here." She finally glanced at the ring and gasped. It was a single rose diamond with a gold band. "It's beautiful, Sloan."

"No, you're beautiful." He placed the ring on her finger, then rose to his feet, carrying her all the way. "Now, I'd like to make you my mate before we start the wedding planning."

"I'm all yours." Becky sighed, hugging his neck.

"Bet your sweet ass you are." He gave her a whack as he carried her to his bed, closing the door with his foot.

******

Blaze pulled into the compound and parked. Heading up the steps to the front door, he looked down and spotted blood splattered all the way up the steps, which then pooled at the door. His senses alert, he stepped over the blood, used his key, and slipped inside.

His eyes followed the trail, but he hesitated and listened. Jill ran from Sloan's office and almost passed him before she realized he was there. Her face was panicked and pinched in rage.

"Oh, God, Blaze." Jill grabbed his arm, pulling him. "It's Katrina."

Blaze didn't say a word, but pushed her to wherever Katrina was. His eyes followed the trail of blood as they ran, his worry for her overwhelming. Jill was heading toward Slade's office. He passed the other Warriors, who were waiting outside in the hallway. Following Jill inside, his eyes landed on Katrina who lay lifelessly on the table. Cuts, bruises, and blood covered her. She was almost unrecognizable.

"She's sedated," Slade said, his voice worried. "I've done all I can do for now. It doesn't look good."

"What the fuck do you mean it doesn't look good?" Blaze's voice was low and deadly. "Why isn't she in the hospital? Anyone else you would have taken, why not her?"

"She can't be moved, Blaze." Slade remained calm. "She's lost too much blood. If I move her now, there's a chance she won't make it. Give it until tonight. If she shows improvement, I'll get her to the hospital."

Blaze couldn't take his eyes off her prone form. Who in the fuck could do something like that to this girl, this sweet woman who would never hurt anyone? "Who did this?" Blaze asked.

"We don't know, yet." Slade's eyes darkened.

"She told me she was going to the vet." Jill sniffed, holding Katrina's hand. "I asked her if she wanted a ride and she said no as she'd be a while because they were allowing her to work off that damn dog's bill so she could take him. She was going to walk some of the dogs and clean kennels. She hoped to work enough today to pay them off and I couldn't break her heart because I knew it would take more than just today. I offered her some money, but she refused and said she was looking forward to it."

"How did she get here?" Blaze still stared at Katrina and the more he stared, the angrier he became.

"I found her on the steps." Jared stood in the open doorway. "Sid checked the monitors and said she walked until she reached the steps, where she crawled the rest of the way."

His eyes shifted to the ground, his fists tightening at his sides. Someone was going to die an ugly death.

"This was pinned to her shirt." Slade handed him a piece of paper.

Blaze took the bloodied paper. Looking down he read the note. WHO WILL BE NEXT? THIS IS JUST THE BEGINNING. was written in bold black letters. Any control Blaze had went straight to hell.

"Get him the fuck out of here," Slade roared as heat came off Blaze in waves.

He felt himself being tackled out of the room, down the hall and outside.

"Jesus!" a voice shouted. "Burned the fuck out of my hand."

"Get away from me!" Blaze roared, his head falling back. He took deep, calming breaths that weren't working worth a shit. He was ready to tear shit up. Fuck!

Everyone listened and stayed the fuck back. Sloan and Becky pulled in, Sloan parking his bike and getting off.

"Keep Becky back!" Jared shouted, running to block her.

"I'm fine!" Blaze dropped his head, but his eyes were swirling and deep red.

"Duncan called me." Sloan reached out, taking Becky's hand. "Where is she?"

"With Slade," Jared answered, but his eyes were still on Blaze.

"We'll find who did this," Sloan said, his eyes on Blaze.

Blaze finally talked himself down. It wasn't easy, but he did it. He turned to Sloan. "Yes, I will." He then headed for his bike. "Stay with her. I'll be back."

"Blaze!" Sloan warned. He handed off Becky to Jared before he stepped in front of Blaze.

"I'm fucking fine," Blaze growled, his eyes going to Sloan's. "I need to do something for her. Now get the fuck out of my way."

"Don't make me regret stepping down," Sloan replied. He then edged away to let Blaze pass.

"Stay with her" was all he said as he jumped on his bike and headed out. As Blaze retraced the steps she would have taken, he kept his eyes out for anything odd that would clue him in on what the fuck happened. Reaching his destination, he walked inside to the counter.

"Can I help you?" the girl asked, staring at his eyes and looking a little afraid.

"We brought a dog in a few nights ago." Blaze glanced around for a familiar face. "I wanted to pay the bill and take the dog."

"Do you have a name?" she asked with a frown.

Fuck! "Ah, Katrina," he said, wishing she would hurry.

"Oh, yes." She tapped something on the computer. "She was supposed to come in today to help. Dr. Reader said she could do that to pay the bill."

"Well, I'm here to pay it in full." Blaze pulled out his wallet. "How much?"

"Five hundred and sixty-five dollars," she replied, then counted the money Blaze put on the counter and printed him a receipt.

"I'll go get him." She took off toward the back and disappeared.

Blaze's anxiety gave him energy that he needed to get rid of, but no bastards who did that to Katrina were around. He swore when he found them, he would kill them in the most painful way he knew how. He paced the waiting room, making everyone inside nervous, but he didn't give a shit.

"Here he is." The girl came out and so did the damn dog, with a white bandage wrapped around its torso.

Blaze wasn't a dog person. He didn't know much about them, but when the dog spotted him his tail began to wag.

"These are his pain meds." She gave him a bottle and handed him the leash. "He needs them every twelve hours with food. And I think that's it. You're good to go."

She knelt down and petted the dog's head. "See you later, Sager."

"Sager?" Blaze frowned, looking at the small dog.

"Yeah, that's the name Katrina gave him. She didn't want him to be in here nameless. He even comes to the name as if he's had it for years."

Blaze actually grinned. "What kind of dog is it?"

"Full-blooded German Shepherd. He's going to be huge. He's only a puppy." She stood, then headed back to the counter. "Good luck. Give us a call if anything happens."

Blaze nodded and headed out the door, the damn dog followed right by his side. Once at the bike, he wondered how in the hell he was going to pull this off. Carefully picking the damn dog up, he stuffed him safely under his shirt, then tucked it in. He pulled his collar down so the dog could peek out. It wasn't the most comfortable thing, but it worked and he only had a short way to go.

"Come, Sager," Blaze said, then chuckled at the name. "Katrina needs you."

Once at the compound, Blaze didn't even take him out of his shirt. He rushed inside and down the hallway to Slade's office. Everyone was still there, even Sloan and Becky. Stepping inside, his eyes went directly to Katrina and then back to Slade.

"She's starting to heal, but it's too soon to tell yet," Slade answered his unasked question.

"Why can't she take my blood?" Blaze finally asked something he should have asked in the first place.

"Because I can't have her healing too fast." Slade frowned down at Katrina. "As far as I can tell, she has nothing broken, but without X-rays, that's not a certainty. We just wait."

Blaze paced toward the table, pulled out his shirt, and lifted the puppy out. He carefully set the puppy down next to Katrina, but was ready to pull him away if he started to get excited. That didn't happen. Everyone watched amazed as the puppy, himself still wounded, carefully leaned over and sniffed Katrina's cheek. He looked toward Blaze, then Katrina, and licked her cheek before curling up and snuggling his head in her neck.

Sitting down in the chair, Blaze put his hand close to Katrina's and wanted to touch her so badly, but didn't. Too many eyes were on them. He looked back to the dog. Something touched his fingers. He turned to see her hand touching his.

Jill began to cry again and left the room. Slade followed, shutting the door and everyone else out.

Taking her hand in his, Blaze rubbed his thumb across a fading bruise on her wrist. "I swear to you I will find who did this." Blaze looked up to her face. "Just don't die on me. You will be revenged."

The damn dog lifted its head, its eyes on his as it growled low in its throat, as if agreeing with him. At that moment, Katrina applied pressure to his hand. A tiny flicker of hope filled Blaze and for the first time that he could remember, he prayed.

Chapter 33

Sloan sat at his desk going through papers. His eyes kept going to Becky, who sat at her computer. He could tell something was wrong and it was driving him crazy. Ever since Katrina had been found beaten and broken on the steps of the compound, Becky had been very quiet, not like herself at all. Actually, the mood around the compound was anything but good. One of their own had been violated, and that they took very seriously.

Again, he glanced up to see her staring at him over her computer. "Becky, are you okay?"

She glanced down for a second before looking back up, her eyes sparkling with tears. "No, not really."

Sloan stood and headed toward her. Gently reaching for her, he pulled her into his arms.

"Is she going to be okay?" Becky said against his chest.

"Slade is taking good care of her." He rested his chin on her head.

Becky was silent for a few seconds. "What you guys do is very dangerous, isn't it?"

Sloan sighed. "Yes, it is." He knew he should have had this conversation with her before things got this far between them, but selfishly he hadn't. "Sometimes things like this happen, but I swear to you, no one will ever touch you," he vowed, his arms tightening around her.

"Sloan, that's not what I'm worried about." Becky stared up at him. "I'm worried about you. Something like that could happen to you."

"Well, they can try," he teased, tilting her chin up higher to look directly into her eyes. "But know that I have something in my life very important to me. I'm going to be one hard son of a bitch to take out."

"Uh, that doesn't make me feel better." She sniffed, but a twitch of her lips made him smile.

"Becky, I promise you nothing will happen to me." Sloan assured her, then kissed her softly. Rising from her lips, he still saw shadows in her eyes. "What else is bothering you?"

Becky hesitated, biting her lip. "I don't know how this is going to work."

This time Sloan pulled back away from her, his face going completely blank of any emotion. "How what is going to work?" His voice was even, his eyes narrowing. He had a feeling he was not going to like what she said next.

"Us," she whispered as a tear fell.

Never had a word gutted him like the word she'd just spoken. For once in his life, he was speechless. He just didn't want to question what she meant, afraid to hear the answer. Sloan Murphy wasn't afraid of a fucking thing. At least, that was the case until she walked into his life.

"I know nothing about you, or your life. I'm human, you aren't." Her voice caught, but she cleared it and went on, "What happens when I start getting older, Sloan? What happens then, when you no longer find me attractive?"

"You will take my blood, Becky. It will keep you young." Sloan felt a little better hearing her problem was just that and not because her feelings had changed for him.

"I have a son, Sloan." Becky's chin wobbled and her eyes filled again. "How is that going to work? A mother's worst fear, my worst fear is losing my son before I die. A mother is supposed to die before her children. I never even took the time to think of this until Katrina. How different we are. How different I am from you."

Her words hit him and he honestly didn't have a solution. For fuck's sake, he stood there like a complete fucking idiot as his life slipped out of his hands. And there was not a fucking thing he could do about it, except stare at her.

"I have to go. I have to think." Becky stepped further away from him, snatching her bag off the table. "I'm so sorry."

"Becky, wait!" Sloan called out, but she was gone and he let her go, for the moment. He would give her only a moment to think and then he would find her.

******

Becky drove in the drizzling rain, happy that Frankie was still in town having dinner with his father before he headed back to school. He agreed to meet with her outside of the restaurant. She had to talk to him. She was confused and needed to talk to her son.

What happened between her and Sloan was fast and furious. One minute she was his secretary and the next she was in his bed, his mate and future wife. All that was fine, other than the fact that she hadn't thought things through. Didn't understand what it meant to be in love with a vampire. Who in the hell would have thought she would have had to consider that one day?

Katrina's condition had sent all sorts of thoughts through her mind and they wouldn't stop. With her feelings for Sloan growing every second, she needed to understand exactly what…. Hell, she didn't know what she needed to understand. She did know she needed to see Frankie.

Pulling up to the restaurant, she got out and texted Frankie. Within minutes he was outside, and she was holding on to her son.

"Mom, you're freaking me out." Frankie hugged her close. "What's wrong? Did something happen?"

Becky told him about Katrina. "I never realized what being in a relationship with a vampire, a Warrior vampire would entail."

"Mom, come on." Frankie frowned at her. "You're tougher than this. What's really going on?"

"I can't stay with him." She shook her head, a few tears escaping, her heart totally breaking. "He will stay the same while I get old. How in the hell can I even think that's okay?"

Frankie laughed, actually chuckled. "Then have him change you into a vampire, Mom."

"Have you lost your mind?" Becky gasped, looking up at him in horror.

"Ah, no, but I think you have." Frankie snorted, then shook his head. "Do you love him, Mom? Actually, let me answer that. Yes, you do. I have never seen you this happy before, ever, and I've known you for a pretty long time. Every single time I've called you, I've wanted to gag because you're disgustingly happy."

"Gag?" Becky frowned at him.

"Yes, gag." Frankie snorted again. "Oh, Sloan did this and Sloan said that." He changed his voice to sound like her.

Becky slapped her hands on her cheeks and stared at her son. "If I change, then I will watch you grow old as I stay the same. I can't do that, Frankie."

"And why not?" Frankie frowned, his eyes narrowing. "Do not use me like this."

"Like what?" Becky gasped, not liking his tone.

"You stayed with Dad for me and you were miserable." Frankie glared at her. "Do not leave a man you love because of me."

Becky fell against her car, her head sinking to her chest. "I never meant to…."

"Knowing how much you love me is enough, Mom." Frankie touched her shoulder before wrapping his arm around her and leaning next to her. "It's time to live your life and let me live mine. Actually, I think it would be awesome to have a vampire for a mom and who knows, I may find a vampire of my own one day. Living forever sounds pretty awesome."

Never could she love someone as much as she loved her son. He was wise beyond his years and seemed wiser than her, which made her damn proud.

"Live your life, Mom." Frankie squeezed her tight.

"How old are you again?" Becky eyed him teasingly.

"I know." He smiled with his chest puffed out. "Pretty freaking mature of me, huh."

"Very," Becky chuckled, then shrugged her shoulders. "This is all new to me. I just don't know what to do."

"Are you going to turn into an old hag tomorrow?" Frankie asked, his eyes shooting over her head at something.

"No," she replied, then laughed because in all honestly, he was right. She had just had a total meltdown for no reason at all. Well, at least a meltdown that could have come later, but she had been truly scared, and her feelings for Sloan were intensifying.

"Just be happy, Mom," Frankie continued. "Sloan's a good guy. I really like him."

"He really is. I think I made a mistake. I hope he understands." She sighed, wiping her eyes.

"Oh, he will." Frankie grinned, looking over her head.

She was getting ready to turn to see what Frankie was looking at, but her ex was coming out of the restaurant and he didn't look happy.

"What in the fuck is going on?" Frank stormed his way toward him. "Dammit, Becky. I've told you when it's my time with Frankie you need to stay the fuck away. Are you that goddamn stupid I have to smack sense into you?"

"Dad." Frankie stepped between his parents. He was smaller than his father, but Sloan wasn't.

"I got this." Sloan stepped in front of both Becky and Frankie. "I'm going to give you one choice and that's only because I respect your son. If you don't turn your ass around and go back into that restaurant, I am going to beat your fucking ass all over this parking lot."

"Who the fuck are you?" Frank actually took a step back, but still tried to sound tough.

"I don't answer to you, motherfucker." Sloan took a step forward. "But if I ever hear you speak to Becky like that again or if you ever even threaten to raise a finger toward her, you will know my rage. You got me?"

Both Becky and Frankie peered around Sloan to see Frank back down. His shoulders drooped as he turned quickly toward the restaurant and disappeared inside.

"Now that was awesome, but it wouldn't have hurt my feelings to see you knock his ass out." Frankie smirked with a shrug. "I know that's pretty shitty to say about my own dad, but he is an asshole most of the time. I only hang with him because if I don't, he makes it hard on Mom."

"Well, you don't have to worry about that anymore," Sloan replied as he turned. "He won't be doing anything to your mother."

Frankie stuck his hand out and Sloan gave it a firm shake. He then grabbed Becky in a tight hug, laughing at her confused look at Sloan. "He gave me his number the day I met you guys for lunch. I texted him after talking to you on the phone."

"I love you." Becky hugged him with everything she had.

"I love ya, mom." Frankie pulled away and smiled first at her, then Sloan. "You belong with him. Now, I'm going to go in, get my shit, and then I'm out. I'll text you when I make it back to campus."

"Be careful!" Becky watched her son head back to the restaurant, tears leaking again.

"He's right you know." Sloan's deep voice surrounded her. "You belong to me."

Becky smiled. "He said with." She knew at that moment she could never live without him. She threw herself into his arms. "I'm so sorry." She held him tightly. "I just got so confused and afraid. This world is a little different for me."

"We'll figure this out, Becky," Sloan promised as he held her. "I swear I will do whatever I can to make sure you are happy."

"That's not going to be hard to do, Sloan, because I am happy. Very happy." She stood on her tiptoes and kissed him on the chin. "I just had a meltdown for a second."

"Red hair thing?" He kissed her back, his mouth curving into a teasing smile.

"A heart thing," she replied, then let him lead her toward his bike. "Hey, what about the car?"

"One of the guys will pick it up. I'm taking you home." Once Sloan mounted the bike, he looked at her before she climbed on behind him. "And never forget, you do belong to me, Becky. You are mine."

She slid on the back of his bike, her arms wrapping tightly around him as she pressed her cheek against his back. "I am yours, Sloan Murphy. I'm sorry I left like that."

"You did what you had to do, Becky. You're an amazing mother." He reached around, shifting her onto his lap while sitting on the bike. "You are an amazing woman. I would have found you, even without Frankie's text. I'm not letting you go."

She put her hand against his cheek, her eyes meeting his. "I don't want to be let go."

"Good to hear." He gave her a wink. "Now, how about we go back to our place to make up?"

"Make up?" Becky frowned as he helped her slide to the back. "We didn't really fight."

"That's a shame." Sloan started the bike. "I've heard make-up sex is the best."

A smile lit Becky's face. "Well, I guess maybe we did have a little fight."

"That's my girl." Sloan gave her a sexy grin over his shoulder before taking off.

Becky sighed, wrapping her arms around him tightly. With an evil grin, she let her hand travel down to his waist and head toward what she had thought about grabbing the previous times she had ridden behind him.

"Son of a bitch." The bike weaved as he grabbed her hand, moving it quickly back to where it should be. "Becky, stop! Dammit, I almost wrecked. You are definitely going to pay for that."

"Promise?" she replied, then squeezed him tighter, moving as close as she could to him.

His only response was a growl as the bike sped up and they flew down the road with Becky smiling and finally feeling at peace.

AUTHOR NOTE

I have so many projects coming up and I'm so excited. I'm finishing up Blaze for you guys as well as starting a new vamp series. Yes, I'm that crazy. The Enforcer is part of the Taming The Vampire box set to be released October 31, 2016. Because of the overwhelming response from beta's I have decided to do a second book. Actually I fell in love with this story and I hope you will also. It is short because of the word limit given to each author in the box set, but I still think you will enjoy and the second will be longer, of course.

I haven't forgotten about the sexy wolves. I still have to write Markus and Dell's stories. So yes, I will be very busy, but that is fine with me. Absolutely love what I do and I thank you all for allowing me to do it.
Hugs!!

COMING SOON

'The Protectors Series' Book #10 Blaze

'Lee County Wolves' Book #3

The Enforcer Book #1 October 31

Find out more about me and the Warriors at

www.teresagabelman.com

Printed in Poland
by Amazon Fulfillment
Poland Sp. z o.o., Wrocław